The

Next Generation

To Mama Raised A Killer

By

Mark Saint Cyr

Library of Congress Control Number:
098274823x

ISBN: 978 0 9827 4823 7

This book was printed in the United States of America.

Published by Atg Tech Publishing Company

To order any books by

Mark Saint Cyr contact:

web-site
www.atgtechpublising.com

e-mail
mrkii@att.net

Atg Technologies & Publishing
P O BOX 40422
Redford, Michigan 48240

A division of
Atg Technologies and Filmworks,LLC

Acknowledgements

I give all praise to the Lord Jesus Christ who gave me the gift to write. I thank him for giving me the foundation to stand on when times were rough through the strength of my parents, now deceased, Ethel Jeanette Smith and Douglas Lee Smith. I hope that through my writing I bring a little relaxation and comfort to my readers. I would also like to thank those readers that keep my dream alive by reading my works. It always fore fills me with joy to know that a character I developed in my mind has made others enjoy the characters life struggles. I will continue to try to give you the reader something that is real and part of reality.

Thank you to you, the people the reader that motivates me to continue writing.

Mark Saint Cyr

Excerpt From

Mama Raised A Killer, The Finale

"What's your fucking name." she asked. "Chris Gucci" he said nervously then he pissed on himself. Cye fired two shots and he fell against the glass of the two way mirror. When Nicky walked in the other room she had picked up that one of us was Reggie's woman. "Terry" she said and tried to hug him to play it off. So she wouldn't lay dead with the rest of the guys in the room.

"Bitch you better get up off of me." Terry raised his gun. "I should blow your ass away from here but I don't want my son to be motherless like my nephew is." He pushed her away. She walked over to Mark Gucci and kicked him in his nuts. Then she spit on him and went to get her belongings. Cye looked at her as she walked by her. Everybody was waiting on me to see what I wanted to do with Mark Gucci. Terry was lighting his cigarettes and putting them out on Mark Gucci's face. He looked at Mark and asked him "Why you kill my sister." Mark Gucci didn't say a word. He didn't even scream when Terry was putting out the cigarettes on his face. The six guys we came with were standing around like soldiers that just completed a mission. They had found a lot guns in the house and some money. They were talking about what they wanted. I came back after looking in all the closets with some coat hangers. Everybody looked at me crazy except Cye. We always know what the other one is going to do. I have missed her by my side when we have to get down like this. Cye went in the kitchen and turned on all the burners on the stove. I found some thick towels and I brought the hanger in the kitchen to Cye. The guys were talking to each other trying to guess what we were about to do. I untwisted the hangers and doubled them so that the part I held was strong. I had the top of the hanger that was twisted sticking straight out. Cye took it and put it on the burner. We did four hangers like that. We left them on the stove until the end was fiery hot. Mark Gucci watched us as his mind tried to figure a way out. He was from the old school. He wasn't going to beg or plead. If this was the way his life ended he was going to take it like a true mob man. Cye was the first to bring the hanger in the living room. Terry was now burning Mark Gucci's hands with the cigarette butts. Cye walked in front of Mark and stuck him with the hot hanger. Mark screamed in agony. She took it out and stuck it in again. Mark screamed again. The pain he felt was like a hot bullet entering his body. I came out the kitchen with my hanger and stuck Mark with it. I twisted it and looked in his eyes.

"This is for my sister" I said and pulled it out and stuck in his stomach again. Reggie came out the kitchen with a hanger. Everybody watched him as he looked at Mark with tears in his eyes. This is for my baby mama. He stuck it in Mark Gucci's throat.

"This is for my son that won't see his mama again." Reggie said. Mark tried to scream but the hanger lodged in his throat wouldn't let him. I hadn't notice Terry was in the kitchen with Cye. When he came out he looked at Mark with his hanger in his hand. All the guys were watching Terry to see where he would put the hanger. They didn't notice the pile of bodies on the floor was moving. One of Mark's men was still alive. He slowly pushed the dead bodies on top of him off. I put my hand around my brothers' shoulders. I knew he needed closure. With tears in his eyes he was getting ready to stick Mark. Mark looked in my eyes as Terry looked in his eyes. He must have looked at me and saw his dead family flash through his mind. The person responsible was me standing in front of him. His eyes squinted. He somehow gained the strength to lunge at me with his knife that came out of the sleeve of his jacket. He stuck me twice real fast. At the same time Terry put the hot hanger through his left eye. Shots started blazing. Mark's guy on the floor had his finger on the A-K automatic and was pointing where he had heard the noise. His body was still under the other men who got shot earlier. Reggie, Cye and the rest of the guys unloaded numerous rounds into the bodies on the floor. Reggie had the guys take each body off each other and they shot everyone in the head. Time went slow for me. I had two stinging feelings in my back and the knife wounds under my heart with Mark Gucci lying on top of me. The last thing I remember was Cye crying.

"Teeka don't you die on me over and over." I passed out. When the smoked cleared my brother Terry was dead along with Mark Gucci and seven white guys, Big brown that came with us and Darryl who was in the basement. They rushed me to the hospital. I remember seeing my husband Mac's face with tears in his eyes as they pushed me down the hall to surgery.

Chapter 1 The Next Generation

I started my day out like I normally do by rolling me a blunt. My breakfast as I say. My days don't start right if I don't get my early morning breakfast. I know it stagnates your mind but my mind is so twisted it doesn't matter any way. I saw my mother get bludgeon to death and my father was killed by my stepmother who is now in a mental institution. I was raised by my Aunt Teeka who ran her own drug empire. So my life has a few options. Don't get me wrong my aunt wanted me to go to college. My life could have went in another direction if I had listened. She even had an escrow account set up for me and my sisters. Four years paid for at any college I choose. But the streets called me when I was eighteen and I was up for the challenge. I had talks with my aunt and uncle Mac that raised me. Both wanted me to go to college but what happened one day changed my life. I remember that day. My homeboy Rick and I went out with our girls. We went shopping at Eastland mall.

Then to the movies and had dinner at Applebees. When we were ready to leave I gave Rick my keys to my car. I went with my girl who had to go to the restroom. When we got back to the car we found Rick was sitting there dead he had been shot in the head and my cousin his girlfriend was gone. We called the police and I called my Aunt Teeka. Within minutes four car loads of guys were at the restaurant. Aunt Teeka was hysterical. My cousin Carletha was her daughter. Uncle Mac who is a lawyer talked to the police as the guys in the cars search the area around the restaurant. The police took my girl and I down to the precinct and questioned us for hours. I remember looking out the back of the police cruiser and saw my Aunt fall to the ground as we were leaving the scene. Rick's cold face and the bullet hole in the middle of his forehead would haunt me for years. Tears formed in my eyes as my girl Terisa comforted me by putting my head on her shoulders. I don't know what came over me that day but I knew I had had enough. I knew one day I would find the person that killed my mother, my best friend and my cousin. When I got home late that evening there were cars everywhere. The circled driveway had cars on it and the lawn was full with expensive cars. It must have been fifty people in the house. We stayed in Gross Pointe an exclusive neighborhood in the suburbs. I could see the white neighbors peeking out their windows. When I got inside guys were everywhere with guns in their waste or AK Automatic rifles in their hands. Uncle Mac led me to the back family room where Aunt Teeka was talking to the kids. I would have thought that she would be lying down trying to relax or crying somewhere. But her mind was steady moving. In the room were my half sisters, identical twins Jada and Jaden and my cousin Aunt Teeka's other child Junior. He was sixteen years old four months younger then my sisters who just turned seventeen. My Aunt was serious and stoned face when she told us all about her and my stepmother's life as a child. Then she told us about her life as an adult. She didn't hold back anything she told us how her parents raised her and how she didn't want any of us caught up in the mistakes she made in her life. She told us how she had killed the Gucci brothers that killed her boyfriend and how the Gucci family had killed her mother and my stepmothers' parents in California. All of us listened as she went through every detail of how they were on top of the drug game and then how they were on the streets with nothing. The one thing that she kept saying was how strong her love for her cousin Cye was. How to the end they were always there for each other. How there was no bond greater than family. She looked at each one of us and said "this is our family. The five of you should not let anything or anyone come between you." The tears formed in her eyes as she thought about the fifth person not there her daughter Carletha.

"No man or woman, no money, no drugs. Not any materialistic thing should ever come between any of you guys." She repeated again. "You guys have to protect each other even when no one else is around." Her strong voice seemed to fade a little when she put her hands on her stomach which was starting to bubble. The phone rang simultaneously as she bent over in pain. Uncle Mac answered the phone.

"What? Which one? We will be right there." At this point there was no more trying to protect the kids we were now adults and everything that went on form this point on we would know about it and be involved with it.

"Carletha's been found. She was found in an alley with her throat cut. A homeless man watched as they dumped her there and called police. They got her to the hospital she is still

alive." Uncle Mac said as he helped his wife stand up. They hurried arm in arm to the car as Uncle Mac shouted out orders to the other men in and around the house. All the kids got in Junior's car and we followed the caravan of cars racing through the streets. I really felt for any police man who would have stopped them. I'm sure there would have been a gun battle. These men were already mad and would have loved to take their frustration out on any brave policeman that stopped any of the ten cars flying down the streets. I looked in the rear view mirror and I saw Juniors eyes while he was driving .They looked so deadly. He had just started his senior year in school and was a good athlete. But I could look in his eyes and see school wasn't going to be a priority for him in the coming future.
"We all have to stick together" I said as I started the conversation. Jada who was the no nonsense person on the group looked at me and said

"What we going to do? These people could be looking for us. It was your car RJ. They could have thought Rick was you. You two like alike and dress alike." Before that moment I hadn't even thought about that. They could be looking for me and all of us. It might be the people that killed my mother and my uncle Terry that was murdered. The car was silent for the rest of the drive. Everybody was deep in their own thoughts. I looked around at all my family in the car and thought about how we were all related. We all grew up in the same household with Aunt Teeka and Uncle Mac. I started living with my Aunt after my stepmother killed my dad. Before that I lived with my dad and stepmother with my half sisters Jada and Jaden next door to Aunt Teeka. Junior and Carletha are my cousins because my mother Tanesha and Aunt Teeka were sisters. We all went to school together and Carletha and I protected the younger ones in school. We were always together. We went to schools where we were the minority. Most of the students were white. The cars stopped and everybody got out and rushed into the emergency room. The nurse panicked and called security. They took Aunt Teeka and Uncle Mac in the back as they hustled us into a waiting room. We waited about an hour before I heard my Aunt Teeka yelling "No, No, not my baby. No, no." Junior burst through the double doors with me and the twins' right behind him.

"Mama what's wrong with Carletha?" grabbing her and holding her tight "What's wrong mama" Junior said through teary eyes. Uncle Mac was shaking his head trying to be strong and not let the tears roll down his face. He held onto the twins and told us Carletha had her throat cut and the same person cut her tongue out. We all stood there in the hallway crying and holding each other. No one said anything I guess they could see we were upset and they gave us our space to console each other. The doctors came out of the room and approached us. Uncle Mac told him these were the rest of their children. So the doctor took us in a room and spoke to us about Carletha's injuries. He told us truthfully that he didn't think she would be able to speak again and that she needed sixty five stitches in her throat. He also said that she was fortunate the homeless guy saw her or she would have died. He also said that whoever cut her tongue out put it in her pocket. She is in surgery trying to get it reattached. He said she will be in surgery five hours so he suggested that we go home and try to get some rest. Aunt Teeka said she wasn't leaving. So the doctor led us to a doctor's conference room that had couches and chairs. No one wanted to leave. Uncle Mac went to the store to get us something to eat. Aunt Teeka looked at each one of us wiped her tears and told us she wasn't finish with her story. We all sat closer to her so we could hear the rest of the story. She told her how her cousin Cye, Jaden and Jada's mother and my stepmother had went crazy killing all the Gucci family members she came in contact with in California. She even cut off one of their family member's dick off and sent it to his father in a jar. Jada and Jaden gasped in horror hearing what their mother was capable of doing. Aunt Teeka stressed that all this was because of the love and the strength of her family ties with her mother and father. Aunt Teeka told us that Cye and her made a death pact. That they would not leave California until all the Gucci family members were dead. She said a lot of her loyal friends died helping them.. She got to the part of how a Gucci brother killed my mother. She looked straight at me and said they slaughtered her in front of RJ. The other kids didn't know that. That was the first time they heard that. It wasn't something that was talked about. My chest built up with anger and tears entered my eyes as I continued to listen. She told us that she didn't want us to get caught up in this but it seemed that it has followed her to the next generation. She looked at each one of us and told us she didn't want us to sell drugs or get into the fast life. But she also said that if we choose that life style she would prefer to give all her knowledge to us then we find out from trial and error in the streets. We all hugged Aunt Teeka and told her we understand and we will always be united as a family. After Carletha got out of surgery we all went in to visit her. We looked at all the tubes coming out of her body and bandages wrapped around her swollen face and we all were in tears. Uncle Mac came in and looked at his family in tears and he just hugged his son and said everything is going to be alright. Aunt Teeka gained some strength from somewhere and told us all.

"Carletha is going to be alright. She has a loving family and we will not leave her side until she gets better." From that day and for the next six months somebody was always by Carletha's bedside. We took shifts. Aunt Teeka and Uncle Mac stayed at night. Junior and I did the morning shift so the twins could go to school and the twins stayed the afternoon shift. They did their homework we played cards a lot of time Junior and I would stay in the afternoon with the twins. We talked to each other and included Carletha in our games even though see couldn't talk. After a while she was getting better and couldn't wait until we came to cheer her up. The five of us bonded together more in those six months then we had growing up together for years. Carletha left the hospital after a year and all the doctors thought it was a miracle. Her vocal cords weren't cut when her throat was cut and her tongue was reattached and healing back in place. She still had to eat liquids and drink through a straw. She didn't talk much put she tried to call our names to get our attention. Doctors said they didn't know if she would be able to talk or not. But it was a good sign she was trying. Carletha had therapist come to the house everyday and soon she was talking slowly. Carletha started getting a lot better and we all started hanging out together again.

Jaden, Jada and myself went to mental hospital to see Mama Cye their mother and my stepmother. They talked to her about what happen even though it seemed she wasn't listening. We told her how hurt Teeka was about everything that was going on and she looked at us and asked "Is Teeka alright? We were all surprised she hadn't talked in years since my daddy died. Weeks went by and she started getting better and better. Now when we went to see her we could talk to her and get her to respond. After a year they released her and Mama Cye came back home. Aunt Teeka was so glad to see her I think they hugged each other for an hour. Our family was coming back together. All of the kids had tears in their eyes. We were all glad to see Mama Cye home. Mama Cye and Aunt Teeka told us stories about them growing up. They were doing more reminiscent then telling us stories. Every Sunday our family would have dinner together at Momma Cye's house or next door at Aunt Teeka's house. It really felt good for me to be part of a family. I never had much of a family. My mother was the only family I knew when I was young. I only remember going to a funeral with my mom. She told me that my grandfather had died. I think I was about eight or nine. All I could remember was his odd name "Tbow."

Chapter 2

By the time I turned twenty five and Junior was twenty one we had our hustle going on. Aunt Teeka was true to her word and schooled Junior and myself whenever we had a problem. After a year we began to grow and the girls wanted in the business. Mama Cye was against it. She didn't want her daughters caught up in the street life. Aunt Teeka told her that she really couldn't stop them. All she could do is guide them and give them her knowledge. Momma Cye sent the girls off to college in Florida. Uncle Mac left town for a few days and when he came back he got us together for a family meeting. He told us he had been in California checking out the Gucci family line. That way we could see what we had coming at us. Uncle Mac really wanted all of us to move to Hawaii. But Aunt Teeka was against it. Now that we were starting to come up in the game she knew she wouldn't leave us here alone. Uncle Mac had pictures of all the Gucci kids and grandkids. He knew their ages and he even knew if they were in the game. He said that three nephews had set up business in Michigan. He said that the Gucci family still controlled the West coast drug trade. Aunt Teeka gave all of us copies of each Gucci family member. Everybody noticed Carletha'a reaction on one picture. She stared at the picture. Her face got cold and stoned she froze. Aunt Teeka went behind Carletha and touched her shoulder tenderly. She then looked at the picture. She looked into her daughters eyes. If her look could talk one would know that death was on her mind. She told us to memorize all the pictures. Make sure that you can recognize any one on the pictures because they are only going to do harm to you if you cross their paths. She told us to always be on the defense, always look over your shoulders and always have each other back. Uncle Mac went back and forth to California and always came back with some information on the Gucci family. I really enjoyed when Aunt Teeka talked to us. She was always real and told it like it was. I got close to Aunt

Teeka when I went to her for advice. I never told anyone but the first time I was challenged on the street Aunt Teeka told me how to handle him next time I saw him. Our business was growing and this older guy from the neighborhood tried to challenge me. He disrespected me in front of some dealers. A guy name Tom pulled his gun on me and was trying to get his reputation by dogging me. "Look young blood, I don't like you. I don't want to see you around here anymore." He said while holding his gun to his side so I could see it.

"All right man" is all I could say. I didn't have a gun on me and I didn't have any backup. Junior was with some girl and I was by myself. I felt like trying to take the guy on. But before I said anything else this older guy walked in front of me and looked at the guy. I hadn't seen him before.

"You better fuck with somebody else. You got a problem with him? This here is my man, you better fuck with somebody else."

"Naw man, I just don't like him" Tom said as he put his gun up. He didn't want any part of the guy in front of him. He had heard of how he killed people back in the day. Tom gave me a look and I knew that if he saw me again he would handle his business. Then he left. I just looked at him and walked away. I told Aunt Teeka about it but she had already got a call from a friend who use to work for my dad Reggie. The next day she took Junior, Carletha and I out to a deserted road. As she drove she was fuming mad. She told us that she had been preaching to us to have each other's back at all times. She got on Junior and told him if he wanted to be a pussy then get out the game and chase women and pussy. She told Carletha that she was sorry that her life was caught in the middle of a family war. But in order to protect her she couldn't be sheltered. She had a choice to stay with the family or go live with her Aunt Bea. Carletha wanted to stay with her mother and deal with anything that came with the family. She laid the law on me. She told me not to go anywhere by myself and don't try to be bigger than the game you in. That's how people get killed she said. Aunt Teeka yelled and yelled at us about unity and family all the way to her destination. The long drive gave all of us something to think about. We would never forget that day. We arrived at a secluded place with nothing but land around. Carletha jumped out like she had been there before. Junior and I looked at Aunt Teeka strange. Aunt Teeka popped the trunk on her Mercedes. She walked to the back of the car where Carletha already had her hands on two small automatic guns. She grabbed a hand full of clips and started loading her guns.

"What you guys waiting for" Aunt Teeka said as she pushed guns in both our hands. She told all of us. "I want you to learn these guns and carry them like there your wallets. You can't be halfway selling drugs or halfway in the game. You must be willing to do what is necessary for you to stay alive and grow. Even if it means killing someone before they kill you. These guns speak for you. Never pull a gun out unless you going to use it. There are no second chances or no do over's. If someone threatens you no matter how minor it is you have to show your strength. Don't leave any business behind. Because that same person you left behind will come back on you and do you harm when they catch you slipping. Do you all understand? We all shook our heads.

"Now" she said looking at Carletha. "Tell me about what you holding."

"I have a nine millimeter automatic with a twelve round clip that holds one in the chamber. I have two extra clips that give me twenty four more rounds. That means I have a total of thirty seven bullets for this gun. I also have a 380 automatic with nine in the clip and I have three extra clips. Total of twenty seven rounds plus the one I have in the chamber I got twenty eight times to kill who I need to." I just looked at Carletha. Was this the same girl that good barely talk because her throat was slashed. I looked at her different for the first time. I hadn't noticed how much she looked like Aunt Teeka. Now she was beginning to act like her.

"Can you boys tell me what kind of gun you holding" Aunt Teeka asked.

"I think I have a nine millimeter with two clips."

"You have a 45 millimeter automatic with a sixteen clip magazine. You have two clips and one bullet in the chamber how many rounds you got." Carletha asked sounding like a pro. I wondered how long she been coming out here. I made a mental note to ask my cousin when I get her by herself. I counted up the bullets in my head and said.

"Thirty three round." I said proudly as Aunt Teeka looked at me with discuss.

"RJ you have a clip in the gun plus the two extra that's forty eight plus one. It's important to know your weapons. Know what they can do so you can protect yourself and each other." Junior looked away when he was asked what he had he just said he did not know. Aunt Teeka took us out further in the fields. She taught us how to shoot the guns, hold the guns and hide the guns. My cousin Carletha was a good shooter. She always hit the mark she never missed. Junior and I got better as we spent more time at the field. After a couple of months we were all good shots. Aunt Teeka took us out twice a week and each of us was looking forward to each trip. On ever ride she would school us on her trials and tribulations in the game. A don't know if we all were eager to go for because the learning of the guns or the stories she would tell us. She had promised us if we learned the weapons and had the patients to care a gun, that she would give us the guns. We all got closer because we were together so much but we started to think a lot because of the thoughts Aunt Teeka was putting in our heads. She was showing us devotion and dedication by putting us together wanting the same cause. That I think was the lesson. We were like the three musketeers we stayed together. When I had a chance to talk to my cousin alone she confided in me. She told me she had been raped and left in the alley for dead. She said she would never forget the face of the men that raped her. She showed me the pictures that she kept with her at all times. I begin to see why her mental state had changed. I told her I would always be there for her no matter what the cause. I told her if needed I would die for her. Carletha had tears in her eyes. I hugged my cousin and she started crying softly. She said she couldn't sleep without seeing the face of the men that raped her. Her attitude on life had changed since that night. Every time she fells the scar on her neck she gets angry. I didn't know what drove her but she knew one day that person would have to pay the piper for what he did to her. Carletha and I went out to get something to eat. Junior said he would meet us at the restaurant. We went to Steve's Soul food Restaurant to get something to eat. We parked the car on a side street and headed towards Grand River. We were walking and talking and I didn't notice a guy crossing the street. When I caught his vision he was in front the restaurant and I thought he was going in. Before I realized it a sharp pain crossed my fore head and blood came rushing out. It was Tom. He was standing in front of me with his gun out. "Young blood didn't I tell you I didn't want to see you around. I looked around and notice he had two guys with him. Carletha was on my right and some of the blood splattered on her blouse.

"Who's going to pay for my blouse?" Carletha asked in her low voice. Tom had his finger in my face avoiding her.

"Next time I see you I'll do more then hit you. You got me young blood" he said holding his gun to his side. I remembered Aunt Teeka's words . Never pull a gun out unless you going to use it.

"What is your problem, you scared I might take your spot with your connection. It's a lot of money to be made in this city man you can't make it all." I was trying to get to my gun under my shirt. Carletha read my mind. She jumped in front of the Tom.

"Who is going to pay for my blouse?" She asked rather loudly. Tom looked at her up and down.

"Bitch you better get the fuck out my face" he yelled as the other two guys laughed. Tom looked back at the other guys and also begun laughing and for a split second he let his guard down. Carletha pulled her 380 automatic out of her pocket and pulled the trigger twice before anybody noticed she had a gun. The two bullets caught Tom twice in his head. His body fell on his stomach and his head hit the concrete with a thump. Carletha turned the gun towards the other guys who were caught off guard. I had my gun out by then and had it also aimed at Tom's two friends.

"You brothers going to pay for my blouse?" Carletha asked in her low normal voice. She had her gun to her side. The two scared man dug in their pockets hastily and gave her a hundred dollars each. "What you want to do cuz? You wanna let this slide or should we take it all the way?" She stood there with her gun pointed at the two men knowing she could drop both of them before they had a chance to reach for their guns if they had one. Before I could answer one of the men fell to the ground. Junior was on top of him with his gun out.

"What's up you guys got beef with these brothers?" he asked us as he cocked his gun ready to kill the guy on the ground. Both men didn't know what to do they were just old friends playing basketball with Tom. Now his mouth got them in some bull shit.

"Man we ain't got nothing to do with what he talking about. We were just going to eat with him. We just got through hooping and we won some money on the game. I'm sorry man I didn't mean to disrespect you or your woman."

"That's my sister and brother and I know you didn't see anything happen here. Now get the fuck out of here before I let her continue unloading her gun." The guy standing picked his friend up and they walked down the street and didn't look back.

"Let's get out of here" I said as we rushed back to the car. Junior jumped in with us and we all took a sign of relieve.

"Carletha I'm glad you're my fam."

"We ride together we die together" she said with a blank look. This was the first time she shot some body and we all knew there was no turning back now. Our life had changed in one hour. Only the man upstairs will know how long that will be.

"Carletha you are lethal. That's your nick name now we going to call you Letha. But only we will know the real reason everybody else will think that's part of your name." Junior and I laughed but Letha remained serious. Sometimes I wonder what she thinks so hard about. Little did I know she was just like her mother beautiful and deadly.

Chapter 3

The word somehow got back to the streets and people started to look at us a little different. RJL is what we called our crew and we started to recruit members or employees. Letha ran the operations with the help of her mother Teeka . She got the connections and we grew in a few months. Since we had a major dealer supplying us drugs as a favor for Aunt Teeka . We keep our prices low and our weight on the packages high. Momma Cye wasn't happy about what we were doing so she sent the twins off to college in Florida. Jaden and Jada kept in touch with us we talked daily. We opened up three drug houses in Detroit two on the eastside and one on the west side. We supplied each with three guys to run it. One person would come to the distribution house to pick up packages when they run out. They had to call in advance and wait for a call back to pick up the packages. We had this set up so that we could control the times eliminating any body trying to set us up. We stamped RJL on all our bags and changed colors of the bags every week. RJL was doing well and word of mouth had crack heads coming from the suburbs to get our product. That meant we were always packaging and distributing. Junior and I were the distributors as Letha made sure she was on top of coping and taking care of the money. Within six months we were pulling in almost ten grand a week profit. We made twenty five hundred each and paid our staff. We put a thousand in the bank for safe money. This happened for two months before we had an issue. Junior was supposed to be at the distribution house at one o'clock. He called me ten minutes after and said he was running late. I called Letha and she said she was on her way. We didn't usually have Letha there in case something happen all three of us wouldn't get caught up. Junior unlocked the door as I reached for my gun. He came in laughing. "Hold on RJ, it's me and my lady." There was an unwritten law not to bring anybody to the distribution house.

"Who is this?" I asked giving him a disapproving look.

"This Sada my lady" Junior said proudly. A knock at the door got my adrenalin running. I cocked my gun and went to the door. His woman looked scared and got behind Junior as I peeked through the door. I saw Dwayne one of our workers so I unlocked the three locks and opened the door. Dwayne came in with two other men following him. One had a gun to Dwayne's head. The men had masked on. One of the men had an assault rifle. He looked at me and said.

"Don't nobody move. You put the gun down" we had got caught. The one with the assault weapon took my gun and then told Junior to put his gun on the table. Junior said he didn't have a gun. The man's eyes looked at the woman behind Junior. She nodded yes and stepped away from Junior. The spark on the barrel of his rifle let off two rounds as Junior fell to the floor screaming.

"You shot me" Junior yelled as he grabbed his stomach.

"Where is the money?" I was looking at Junior on the floor then I felt a hard cold piece of steel explode on my head. I fell to the ground holding my head as blood poured into my hand.

"The money is in the bag in the bedroom" one of the guys went in the bedroom to retrieve the bag. When he came back he told me to empty my pockets. I felt a little better because I had went to the bank today. It was Saturday and we usually split our money on Fridays. I emptied my pockets and tried to look at the perpetrators eyes to get some glue to who he was. He took the five hundred dollars I had on me to give Momma Cye. Then the girl emptied Junior's pockets. Junior looked astonished while holding his bleeding stomach.

"Sada you set me up?" Junior was fading in and out.

"She didn't set you up mother fucker, I did" The guy with the assault weopon said while counting the money the girl gave him.

"I was going to kill your ass for fucking my girl, but this here ten thousands will due, you can have her." He grabbed the bag kicked Dwayne down and took off without the girl.

"Don't leave me here" Sada said as the two guys burst out the door and jumped in their car and sped off. Sada took off running behind the car. She didn't want to stay and face the consequences. She ran for blocks fast as she could. As she crossed West Seven Mile a car swerved to a stop and just missed her. The scary look in her eyes caught the eye of the driver. They locked eyes for a few seconds then the girl took off running again. It was Letha she almost hit the girl while trying to answer her cell phone.

"Hello what up cus" she said to RJ.

"Juniors been shot call 911"

"Who shot him?"

"We got robbed, call 911, I'll tell you about it when you get here. " I hung up my phone and told Dwayne to leave before my people got here. Letha hung up the phone and pulled up to the house that was two blocks away. Junior was bleeding and unconscious. Letha ran to the bathroom and got some towels. She put pressure on his wound and called his name.

"Junior wake up, Mac Arthur Jr wake up" She yelled to her brother. She pressed the towel on his stomach and the blood temporary stopprd coming out. The towel started felling up with blood as the ambulance arrived. The attendants came in followed by police with their guns out.

"Anybody else in the house" the police asked. I shook my head no as the ambulance attendants worked on Junior. An attendant looked at my wound and asked me if I wanted to go the hospital. I told him no and he put a bandage on my head as they hustled Junior out to the ambulance and rushed to the hospital. The police begin to ask us questions when Aunt Teeka, Momma Cye and Uncle Mac came to the house. Aunt Teeka asked me what hospital they had taken Junior and I told her Bodsfort. We were trying to leave as the police stopped us and told us he needed to ask us some questions. Uncle Mac pulled out his card told the police it was his son and if they had any questions call him. Letha and I tried to get in Letha's car when her mother pulled her arm and told us to ride with them. I knew we had to tell them what happen and why we didn't have each other's back. I just knew Aunt Teeka was going to be upset. I just told her we got stuck up and set up by one of our workers. She didn't say a word. Momma Cye asked a lot of questions and Uncle Mac had some too. I tried to answer them because I was the only one in the house besides Junior. I hope Junior doesn't start talking before

I get a chance to tell him what I told his parents. We arrived at the hospital and they rushed us back to the ER. A doctor came out and said he was in surgery and he should be alright. Only one bullet hit him in his stomach. We stayed in the ER all night. My cell phone was blowing up. All the houses was out of product and they wanted to re up. I went in the hallway and told them we were out until tomorrow and don't call me back. We stayed in the hospital for six hours before the doctor came out to talk to us. He said Junior's surgery went well and he should be alright. They had to remove one of his lungs that was punctured by the bullet. Junior stayed in the hospital for two weeks before he was released. Aunt Teeka and Uncle Mac were arguing all the time. So much that Letha came over to our house instead of going home. She told me that Uncle Mac wanted to take Junior to Florida to live. Aunt Teeka was totally against it. Letha and I continued to run our business. But we never left each other's side. Letha wasn't satisfied with what went down on the day of the robbery. I told her the truth about what happened the day of the robbery. Letha said she has seen the girl who set us up somewhere in the hood. We begin to make our self more visible. We rode around in the hood and watched as our crew did their business. It worked out for us because we could watch them while we still looked for the girl who set us up. We spent at least three days out the week rolling with our crew. We had four dedicated guys and Darnell who wanted Letha bad. They hung out together but he never got a chance to be with her alone. I guess I was a little over protective of my cousin and I was always around. Plus I didn't trust Darnell too much. He didn't grow up in the hood and I had a bad feeling about his loyalty. I had to make a trip to our safe house to pick up more product and I asked Letha to roll with me. She said she wanted to get her hair done and asked if I could drop her at the hair salon and pick her up when I was through with the business. I dropped her off and I headed to the safe house. Letha was met at the door by Bert the salon owner and rushed straight to the sink to get her hair done. Afterwards she sat under the dryer while the owner worked on another girls head. She was sewing weave in her head and she knew it would take longer than it would for Letha's hair to dry. After thirty minutes Bert went and checked on Letha and told her to come so she could finish her hair. She sat Letha in the chair next to the girl's hair she was doing and started working on Letha's hair. She start giving Letha dirty looks and rolling her eyes at her. When Bert was almost done with Letha's hair Sada stood up

"Why the fuck you got me waiting while you work on this bitch hair. I was in here before her"

"Who the fuck you calling a bitch" Letha yelled while she looked around for her purse. She always had her gun and she grabbed her purse.

"Please Letha, I'll take care of this" Bert said knowing Letha's reputation and knowing she runs with drug dealers.

"You heard what I said bitch" the girl said as Bert told her to sit down.

"I'll be finish in a minute" Bert said as Letha sat down with her purse in her lap. She was ready to smack this girl with her gun. Bert looked at Letha with pleading eyes. Letha sat down because of the respect she had for Bert but she kept her eye on the girl. Bert finished her hair while the girl kept mouthing off.

"Yea, you go ahead and finish because I'm going to mess that shit up any way." She threaten then she picked up her cell phone and started dialing.

"It's going to be some trouble up in here"

She said out loud for Letha to hear her. She told her man to come up to the salon.

"Sada that's not necessary. You can get in the chair now" Bert said when she finished Letha's hair. Letha heard the name Sada and the picture of the young lady that she almost hit when Junior was shot came in her mind. She looked at the girl and started to shoot her right there. But she taught about it and texted me. She told me to get some guys and come to the salon that the people who robbed us might be there. Letha sat in her chair staring at the girl who was talking plenty shit.

"Bitch you better get out of here before I'm done. I'm going to stomp a hole in your ass" She was selling wolf tickets she knew her man would be there soon. Letha looked at the girl confidently and smiled while she looked at her hair in the mirror.

"You know what I'm going to wait on you" Letha sat in the chair and started manicuring her nails. She just stared at the girl who was now getting nervous. The door opened and everybody in the salon looked at the door. The tensioned was high. I walked in and sat down to the left of the door. A few minutes later Darnell walked in looked at a magazine and asked if he could get a haircut. The receptionist put his name down and told him to have a seat. Darnell sat close to the receptions desk where Letha was sitting on the other side. Sada didn't notice me even though she had seen me before. I kept me head in a magazine as I watched what was going on. Letha gave me some eye contact to let me know just chill and to follow her lead. I knew she was strapped but I didn't know why she wanted more back up with the guys outside. Sada looked at Letha and watched the door. Bert had just finished her hair when two men walked in and went straight up to where Sada's was sitting.

"What's up girl, why you call me up here?"

"This bitch disrespected me and I'm going to beat her ass" he looked at Letha who looked like she wasn't scared or even cared about what Sada was talking about. Her eyes was on Sada and her hand was in her purse.

"Go ahead and handle your business we got your back" the guy said and backed away and watched as the girl got out the chair and took off her heels.

"My man told me to beat your ass" Sada tried to slap Letha while she was seated. Letha caught her right hand and pushed her to the side as she got up with her gun in her hand. She backhanded her with the butt off her gun as her boy friend reached for his gun.

"Don't move mother fucker" Darnell had his forty five automatic at his head. The other man tried to back out the door when I hit him in his mouth. Blood splattered to the person sitting next to him. I pulled my gun out and told my man to be cool. Everything happened so fast the people inside the salon was in shock.

"Is this your man?" Letha asked Sada. "How long you been with him cause I think I fucked him a few months ago."

"I been with Al for six years" she started crying and yelling. "I know you haven't been fucking around on me with this bitch.

"This ain't about you, you said that you was going to kick my ass. We are going to take this outside. Bert I'm sorry for the bull shit. I'll be back in two weeks for my appointment." Letha pushed Sada towards the door. Darnell turned around and asked if anybody seen anything. Everybody in the salon lowered their heads and continued doing whatever they were doing. We pushed the guys and Sada out to the awaiting van. There was a guy on each side of the door as we came out the salon.

"What's this about" Sada's boyfriend pleaded. " Yaw can't be this tight for some bitch." My gun caught his last word right in the middle of his forehead. The blood poured out as he fell back on the van.

"Nigger don't you cal my sister a bitch again" I put my gun to his head ready to pull the trigger. Letha pulled my arm back.

"Hold up let's get off this corner" we put the three of them in the van. Letha and I got in and I told Darnell to follow us in my car.

"Look man I don't have anything to do with this." The other guy that was with Sada's man said. Letha looked at him and waved her gun for him to shut up. No one said another word. Letha and I were at the back of the van and the three of them was sitting on the side.

"I'll only ask you this onetime Sade, did you use to fuck with Junior?" The three of them was in shock they had no idea that this was about the robbery. They all know that Junior was the guy who was shot.

"I didn't mean for him to get shot. I was just suppose to set him up"

"So you do know my brother" Sade started crying she knew she had been caught. The van was silent the only thing you heard was sobs from Sade wondering what was about to happen. The van came to a sudden stop. The driver and the passenger came around and opened the door for us. We were on the east side in a dilapidated east side neighborhood. No houses were around and we were in an alley. We got out and the drivers pulled the other three out. We all had our guns out as we pushed the three to an abandon garage.

"You guys stuck up my dope house and shot my cousin."

"I didn't have anything to do with it" the other guy yelled and he took off running. Within a split second the scene changed. I raised my gun and fired twice hitting the runner in the leg and the back. Al Sada's boyfriend surprised us by pulling his gun out. He shot and hit the driver of the van as Letha pulled her trigger. The bullet caught his shooting hand as he grimiest in pain. She shot him again in the same arm as he yelled. Blood splattered on Sade's face and she screamed. Al fell to the ground Letha walked over to him looked into his eyes and asked.

"Did you shoot my brother, Junior?"

"Yes I shot him, he was fucking my girl until I caught them then I made her set him up" he somehow tried to show his masculine side. His voice got stronger as the pain of his wounds made his ego gain strength. Letha looked him in his eyes and shot him in his heart. Sade cried she knew her time had come. Letha looked at her.

"I'm I still a bitch?"

"I'm sorry I didn't mean no harm. I really liked Junior, but I knew Al would kill me if I didn't do what he asked."

"The only reason you still walking is because my brother asked us not to take you down. Against my better judgment I'm going to let him handle you. You better get in touch with him. Now get the fuck out of here." Sade backed away and took off running. Letha just shook her head. "That bitch is a track star" she said and we all laughed. We went to check on our driver and he was dead. The guy that ran was dead and Al was dead. We drugged the bodies to the garage and poured some gasoline on them and the garage. Before we set the flame Darnell pulls up. I pulled Letha to the side and asked her what was up with her and Darnell. She said nothing that he was pressing her to hard and asking too many questions about me. I told her it was strange that he didn't take that guy Al's gun away from him at the salon. She looked at me and said whatever you want to do cus I'm down with you. Darnell got out the car and saw the dead bodies in the garage.

"What happen who killed them?"

"He pulled a gun on us that you were supposed to take. Now my boy is dead because of your mistake." Darnell assessed the situation and knew he was in trouble. He felt that he could talk his way out of it with Letha having his back. He put his hand on his gun.

"Letha I know you got my back on this" Darnell begged. Letha pulled her gun at the same time that I did. The other guy already had his gun pointed at Darnell he looked at all of us then removed his hand off his gun.

"Who you working for?" she asked moving close to Darnell.

"I work for you" he responded as Letha shot in the air and the bullet flew just above his head. So much that he could feel the air off the bullet going by.

"Who sent you to work for us. You didn't grow up around here." I was tired of the talk and I shot Darnell in his knee. I walked over to him put my gun to his temple and cocked my gun. He knew he had been made and he knew he was going to die.

"Alright some white guy paid me to get information about you"

"Who, who paid you?"

"I don't know his name" Letha thought for a moment then she pulled a picture from her purse.

"Is this the man?" she asked while holding the picture in his face and her gun to his chest.

"Yea that looks like him. He wanted to know about the operation."

"And you gave him information on us instead of being a loyal soldier to us?" I kicked him down and was getting ready to put him out his misery. Letha said hold on cus let's let him slide. I heard her but I didn't believe her. Aunt Teeka always taught us to never let anyone off so they can come back and get you. I looked in her eyes.

"Let him live, cus." I took his gun out of his waist and kicked him in the nuts. He screamed in pain. Letha moved over and bent down and whispered in Darnell's ear.

"My cousin wants to kill you. The only way I can help you is if you can give us something on the guy who wants information about us."

"I don't have any information on him"

"Ok cus he's all yours, do what you need to"

I cocked my gun and put it to his head

"Wait a minute I'm suppose to meet him tomorrow."

"Hold up cus lets hear what he has to say."

"He was suppose to pay me tomorrow."

"Pay you for what?" Letha asked as she stepped on his angle that the bullet had gone right through. Darnell yelled in pain. Trying to grab his leg. Letha put more pressure on it. Blood formed around her shoe as the pain shot up to Darnell's brain. He screamed in pain.

"Pay you for what, what you tell him?" Letha took her foot off his wound.

"He's was paying me for the robbery." Darnell knew it was over for him but he really liked Letha so he gave her the only thing he could. "We were paid to rob you, but you were supposed to be at the house. I'm sorry but I thought that I could get close to you and do what I was paid twenty thousand for." Before Letha pulled the trigger he yelled.

"Wait I suppose to meet him today on the Westside."

"Where at?"

"At the Little Caesar's Pizza on Seven Mile Road."

"What time?"

"Around six o'clock. He won't come if he doesn't see me."
Letha put her gun down as she thought for a minute. She told me to put him in the van. Letha took his cell phone as my other soldier and I put him in the van. We drove back on the Westside to the safe house. We pulled Darnell out of the van took him in the house and bandaged him up. I looked him in his eyes and told him.

"If you do anything stupid I will kill you and then go looking for your family." Darnell looked up through the pain he felt in his leg. Teary eyed he shook his head that he understood. We tied Darnell up and duck taped his mouth. I called two more men to help watch him. Letha and I left and went home to change and to get more arsenals.

Chapter 4

When we got to the house we found Letha's mother Aunt Teeka in the living room crying. Momma Cye was by her side. "Mama what's wrong" Letha asked as she ran over to her mother's open arms.

"Your step daddy packed his clothes took Junior and left" Momma Cye said harshly. Aunt Teeka didn't say anything she just hugged her daughter tightly. I knew their marriage was on the rocks. Uncle Mac was never home and Aunt Teeka spent most of her time over our house with Momma Cye. They were always talking about men and the past. They both were acting like their life's had no importance. I really felt sorry for both of them.

"Mama you ok, I'm sorry about what's going on but I really need to talk to you."

"I'm ok, Carletha I knew this was coming . I knew your daddy would leave I just didn't know how to prepare for it."

"I'm going next door Teeka I'll talk to you later" Momma Cye said as she got up to go.

"Wait Aunt Cye you need to hear this too"

"Yea Momma Cye we need to find out how you feel about this." I said to my step mother.

"About what, what's wrong" Aunt Teeka temporarily forgot her husband had left her. Her interest was now on her daughter. "What happen Carletha and I don't want you to leave anything out." Letha explained what happened and how we took care of it. Her mother's eyes lit up when she mentioned the white man that we were suppose to meet. When Letha showed her the picture of the man I could see the vengeful look in her eyes and Momma Cye's eyes. They looked at each other and if their eyes could talk you would know that they weren't going to let us go at this alone. Letha put the icing on the cake when she looked at her mother and said.

"Mama this is the man that raped me" tears ran down her cheeks. Her hand touched the scar on her neck compliments of the man raped her. "He cut my throat and left me for dead." Letha began crying hard and shaking.

"I'm sorry baby" was all Aunt Teeka could say. She held her daughter close wiping the tears from her face. Momma Cye pulled some Kleenex from her purse and gave them to Letha and hugged her. I stood there with tear in my eyes but I refused to let them fall. I wiped my eyes and also went and hugged my cousin. Aunt Teeka took us all in the basement. She opened a special door that was hidden in the cellar. The room was full of every kind of gun made. We all picked guns and Momma Cye insisted we all had silencer's on them. The next few hours went by fast. Aunt Teeka and Momma Cye were following us in their car. We went to the drop house and they stayed in the car when we went inside the house. Letha questioned Darnell again until his cell phone rang. I put my gun towards his head and told him don't try to get cute and warn the man on the phone. We put the phone on speaker.

"Darnell, this is Tony."

"You got the money you promised me?"

"You got the information I asked you about?" The white voice on the phone asked.

"Yes I got a little more I know where they live." Darnell said looking at me with the gun to his head. He thought that if we get the white man that we would let him walk.

"I will meet you at the usual spot on West Seven Mile."

"I'll be there at seven sharp." Darnell wanted to live and he thought that maybe we wouldn't be able to kill him and the white guys. He knew the white guy always had two or three guys with him. He didn't tell us that but we already had back up. Letha was kind of quiet all the way there. She had a lot on her mind. It's going to be hard for her to face the man that raped her. We pulled up to the Little Caesars three cars deep. I sat in the car with Darnell kneeled down in back seat with my gun on Darnell.

"If you open your mouth and the wrong words come out I'll shoot you first I don't care if I die."

"I'm not going to say anything RJ just let me go man when you get what you want." He was trying to soften me up so he could live another day. My mind was already made up and I know Letha wasn't going to let him live. Aunt Teeka parked her car close to the driveway when you come on the lot. Letha and the other two guys were in the van at the back of the store. Their van was out of the sight of any cars coming on the lot. A white Cadillac STS pulled on the lot. The car pulled up on the side off the building. My cell phone rang.

"There are three men, two in the front one in the back. I think the one in the back is the man we want"

"OK" I hung up and told Darnell to be cool and we all can leave here alive. I wanted to give him some hope. I ducked deeper in the back seat.

"He is motioning for me to come over to him. What you want me to do"

"Go over to him I can still see you. Don't let me have to shoot you in the back of your head." When he opened the door I peeked and saw Aunt Teeka and Momma Cye get out their car.

"Wait a minute. Act like you looking for your cell phone" I told Darnell as I watched Aunt Teeka and Momma Cye go towards the white Cadillac. They wore long coats and it look like they had on dresses. They wore some funny looking hats and they had books in their hands that they kept close to their chest. They walked on each side on the car. The men noticed them walking towards them and put their guns up. They thought they were Jehovah Witnesses.

"Excuse me sir, do you believe in God" Aunt Teeka asked the man. Momma Cye knocked on the other window. Both the white guys in the front looked back at their boss for direction.

"Get rid of them"

"No we are not interested" the guy on the driver's side said through a cracked window.

"Please Sir, can I leave you something to read" again the guys looked back at the boss.

"Take the book so they will leave" he yelled. Both windows were let down by the driver. Aunt Teeka and Momma Cye still had the books close to their heart. They held the books with both hands. The books covered the hand with the gun in it. When the windows were all the way down Momma Cye gave the passenger the book.

"Bless you my child" she said. When she released the book to the man she pulled her 9 millimeter gun with the silencer on it and shot him twice. Aunt Teeka shot the driver the split second he looked over to see the bullets go through the passengers' skull. They both stuck their guns in the windows and told the man in the back don't move.

"What the fuck? I'm Toni Gucci you fucking with the wrong family." The man in the back sit said wiping splattered blood of his face with a handkerchief. When I saw their guns come out I jumped out the car. After I got out I shot Darnell in the back of his head. Letha and the two guys got out of the van with their guns drawn. Toni Gucci sat in the back seat like he wasn't worried about a thing. I looked at him and he was younger than I thought. He was about thirty. He had a smirk on his face. When Letha walked up to the car his smile went away. "Is this that man" Aunt Teeka asked her daughter. Letha looked the man in his eyes.

"Why did you rape me I don't even know you?"

"Your family was responsible for killing my grandparents, my uncles and my cousins. You were suppose to die in that alley you black bitch" Letha started shooting when he said black. By the time he got the bitch out everybody was pumping bullets in his body. Since we all had silencers on our guns all you heard a lot of thumps. His bullet written body slumped in the back sit of the car. I grabbed Letha and pulled her to the car with Aunt Teeka and Momma Cye. We all got in and sped off. Our two men got in the van and left. Aunt Teeka told Letha and me that she didn't think we were strong enough to be in the game. She said that she felt we were going to get killed. She didn't think we had a loyal crew to watch our backs. She also said she and Momma Cye were thinking about getting back in the game. She asked us what we thought. Letha and I looked at each other each in our own thoughts. We were silent on the ride back to the house.

Chapter 5

Uncle Mac and Junior had moved to Florida. Junior called me daily but I never told anybody. He said he didn't want to leave but his Dad made him. He said he didn't like it to much because his Dad was always gone. He spent most of his time at the beach and talking to girls. He asked me when I was going to visit him. I told I couldn't leave. I told him about how his mother and my step mother wanted to help run our business. He thought it was a good idea because no one would protect us better than they could. Plus they had all the connections. Uncle Mac went to a meeting with a client. He was representing her in a murder case. After a few meetings with Dena they started hanging out. Dena set up a meeting with Uncle Mac at a hotel bar a week later. They had a couple of drinks and decided to get something to eat. They went to the restaurant in the hotel and sat across from each other in a booth. Uncle Mac was really feeling Dena. She made him laugh something that he hadn't done in a while. He felt so comfortable around her. She reminded him of his wife Aunt Teeka. They sat and talked. Dena gave Uncle Mac compliments that made him blush. As the evening was winding down Dena took off one of her shoes and started massaging Uncle Mac's inner thighs. It had been months since he had sex so he got exited immediately. Dena felt his manhood with her foot. "What is that you have in your pocket?"

"Something I will be glad to share with you." Uncle make retorted smoothly.

"You sure you want to share all of that with me?"

"If you want it" Uncle Mac said. Dena looked in his eyes as her foot massaged his dick through his pants. Uncle Mac was ready to burst she worked her foot to perfection. She had uncle Mac sweating. He loosen his tie and asked.
"Where do we go from here?" Dena looked at him smiled then reached in her purse and pulled

out a key.

"I'm going to my room to take a shower would you join me?" She got up before he could answer and walked to the elevator. Uncle Mac asked the waiter for the bill then threw a hundred and fifty dollars on the table. He snatched the key up downed the rest of his drink and bolted towards the elevator. The elevator opened and there was Dena. Her blouse was unbutton she must have taken off her bra. Her titty nipples were showing threw her sheer blouse. Uncle Mac could see the formation of her large breast which he couldn't wait to touch. Her skirt seemed a little shorter than it had been in the restaurant. It showed most of her creamy smooth white thighs. Uncle Mac stepped in the elevator and Dena pushed him against the side of the elevator with her body. She kissed him deeply. She was breathing hard when she unbuckled his pants to reach his hard dick. Her breathing was strong as she struggled to pull his dick out. The elevator jumped and started moving up. Dena pressed a button and it stopped in between floors. Uncle Mac put his hand under her skirt and felt her wet vagina and he stuck his finger in it as she moaned of its good feeling. Dena was pulling on his dick so hard it was beginning to hurt. He pulled her blouse open and put his mouth on one of her large breast and his hand on the other. Uncle Mac backed her up and lifted her legs so that she was sitting on the hand rail in the elevator. In one motion he stuck his dick inside her while he sucked on her titties. His movement was slow and methodical. Dena was trying to move but she was in total ecstasy. Her body was shaking and she was clawing on his back. Her finger's dig deeper into the suit jacket and shirt Uncle Mac had on. His trusts were hard and deliberate. He wanted her to remember him. Dena yelled her pleasure."

"Fuck me daddy, fuck me hard MacArthur" she screamed. Uncle Mac was beating that pussy up. Dena had never had a man like him before.

"Daddy fuck me in my ass please. I want you to do me anal" she yelled Dena wanted it all. Uncle Mac spun her around bent her over so her hands touched the elevator floor. He stuck his dick right into her awaiting ass. The moistness of her wet pussy that came four times let Uncle Mac's dick slide right in her already open ass hole. He pulled it out and rammed it in again to the pleasure of Dena.

"Dam" she screamed " it's yours daddy fuck it hard" she yelled and moved with each movement of his. Uncle Mac took it out and stuck it back in her pussy for a minute then back in her ass. Dena loved it she screamed at the top of her lungs the next time he stuck it in. Her body trembled and a mist of sweat poured out her skin. Her blouse was soak and wet. The elevator jumped and started going upwards. Dena and Uncle Mac rushed to put their clothes just as the elevator door opened.

They walked hand in hand to the room. Uncle Mac opened the door with the key. The room was on the top floor and the floor was empty. It was a Monday so the Hotel wasn't busy as usual. Dena stepped in the room and said she needed to take a shower. She went straight to the bathroom and stayed in there for a while. Uncle Mac was a little frustrated. Although the sex was great he did not get satisfied so he was waiting on her so he could finish. He wanted to see how she felt on the bed. He fell to sleep waiting on Dena to get out the bathroom. Uncle Mac was awakened by a cold steel gun jammed against his forehead. When he tried to move four men had him. Two had his feet and two had his hands. He still felt the cold steel on his forehead.

"Be still" someone yelled. He didn't move

Uncle Mac tried to focusing on what was happening to him. He laid there with his feet tied to the bedpost. His hands were tied to headboard. He still was naked and the men in the room sat away from the end of the bed. They didn't want to look at his genitals. Uncle Mac finally begin to focus there were five white men.

"Dena, hurry up and get out here" Dena came out from the bathroom completely dressed."

"It took you guys long enough to get here." Dena had set Uncle Mac up. She was attracted to him. She wasn't suppose to have sex with him put her anticipation got the best of her. She was sorry she set him up. But her family would be proud of her.

"What you guys want from me" They looked at Dena she felt guilty she had fucked him.

"These are my cousins. James Gucci, Tom Gucci, George Gucci III and my brother Leon. I'm Dena Gucci"

"Ok, what does that have to do with me" Uncle Mac asked. He knew that they didn't know he was involved in the family deaths or he would have been dead. Dena went in the bedroom and closed the door. She didn't want to see what was about to happen.

"We know you've been asking questions about

our family. I want to know who you working for or who you giving this information to." All the guys sat in the chairs and whispered to each other.

"I don't know what you talking about ask Dena about me" Uncle Mac was trying to stall. Dena came out the room and sat with her cousins.

"Dena you vouching for him" James asked her.

"I'm not vouching for no one" James pulled his gun and shot Mac in his foot. Dena jumped back. She wished she had a few more rounds with Mac. She thought to herself. What a waist. She was the spoiled freak in the family.

"Who is Teeka and Cye"

"I don't know what you talking about" One of the other cousins shot Uncle Mac in his other foot. He was lying down so the bullet went through his foot and flew right past his cheeks. Uncle Mac braced himself trying to endure the pain.

"Were you here in California when our grandparents and parents were killed? You say you don't know Teeka and you don't live in Gross Pointe Michigan."

"I live in Detroit" the cousins had heard

enough. They all shot him. The bullets struck every part of his body. Uncle Mac last thoughts were of the good times he had with his wife Teeka and his kids. A tear fell from his eyes. His last thoughts were hoping they wouldn't find his wife and kids. He died willingly he always knew someday he'd pay for killing people.

A hard knock at the door woke Junior up. He thought his dad forgot his key. He sat up in the bed of their new condominium and looked at the radio clock. It was four thirty in the morning. He hadn't seen his dad in three days. The knocking got louder. Junior jumped out the bed and looked at his gun on the night stand. He picked it up on his way to the door.

"Who is it"

"Police" Junior put the gun in a end table drawer before answering.

"What you want"

"Are you MacArthur Whitehead Jr."

"Why"

"Sir please let us in. We want to talk to you about your father. I don't want to discuss this in the hallway. Please" the police officer almost begged. Junior opened the door and four large white men came in. All the policemen showed their badges. Two were from the FBI. Junior looked at them strange as they introduced their self's.

"Please have a seat Mr. Whitehead"

"What's this about"

"I'm sorry to tell you that we found your father dead in a hotel room in the downtown area."

"What no, what happened" Junior put his hand in his head and started to cry. All the officers watched his reaction.

"We need to ask you some questions do you mine going downtown." Junior was no dummy he knew the law. His father was a lawyer and they talked a lot about similar situations.

"I'm I a suspect or under arrest for anything." The policeman was a little mad of his response.

"You need to come downtown so we can question you"

"So you telling me I can't call my lawyer or mother. I'm I under arrest?"

"No Mr. Whitehead you are not"

"So I will be downtown with my lawyer to identify my father's body." Junior stood up and went to the door and opened it.

"Your father was shot twenty four times so get your mind ready" One police officer said he couldn't let Junior feel like he got the best of them. Junior slammed the door behind them and dialed his cell phone. His mother answered.

"Mama" he couldn't hold it any longer. He broke down crying.

"What's wrong Junior" Aunt Teeka tried to calm him down so she could find out what happened. She was over our house Momma Cye , Letha and myself was all ears. Finally Junior blurted out.

"Daddy is dead, mama daddy is dead" Aunt Teeka just held the phone and her face showed what we all had been thinking. Momma Cye took the phone out of her hand.

"Junior this your Aunt. Where are you? What did they say about your dad?" Momma Cye listened then she told Junior do not leave that room until we came and got him. She told Letha to go pack a bag for her mother. She then went into the room and made some more phone calls. I was left there with my thoughts. I had a feeling this had something to do with the feud between the two families. I decided that I was going with them so I went in the room and packed a bag. Thirty minutes later Letha was back. Momma Cye was comforting a shocked Aunt Teeka. She told me that she would be back soon and asked me to look after Letha.

"I'm going" Letha said. "I already got my bags packed and it's nothing you can tell me to keep me from going." She looked at her mother and hugged her as she helped them off the couch. "I'm going too Momma Cye my cousin needs me." She just looked at me and Letha standing our ground against our parents. I guess we reminded them so much of themselves. We all hugged each other shaded some tears and left.

We arrived in California in about four hours and took a cab straight to Uncle Mac's condo. When we arrived Jada and Jaden were there along with Aunt Bea momma Cye's sister who was a judge. "What are you girls doing here? You suppose to be in school."

"Mama we had to be with our cousin, we been here for a while." Jada said to her mother. Aunt Bea didn't want the kids to go the morgue but Aunt Teeka said she wanted all her kids by her side. She wanted them to see what this life can do to you. We all went to the police station and downstairs to the morgue. Aunt Bea took Junior upstairs to talk to the detective that came by his house. We went downstairs to the morgue. They put us in the little room with a window. We were huddled around the window when the blinds opened Uncle Mac body was under the sheet. The attendant pulled the sheet from over his head. Aunt Teeka looked but had no reaction. Momma Cye just shook her head. Letha was yelling and trying to get through the window. The twins held her back and hugged her as they cried with her. I stood their frozen. Although I had seen a few dead people in my young life, I had never seen anyone that I actually knew and cared about. Aunt Teeka picked up the phone receiver to talk to the attendant on the other side of the glass.

"Can u please pull the sheet all the way back"

"Are you sure? We haven't prepped him yet"

"Please I want to see my husband one last time"

"Mrs. Whitehead you know he was shot multiple times."

"Yes, please." The attendant pulled the sheet back and Uncle Mac's bullet ridden body was revealed. Aunt Teeka beat on the glass. "I'm sorry Mac, I'm sorry I should have listened." Momma Cye tried to comfort her with tears in her eyes. Letha screamed when she saw her father's body. Jada and Jaden held Letha's arms and I hugged my sisters

"Why mama, why they do this to him" Jada wanted answers. She couldn't believe someone would take the time to put this many bullets in someone that they knew was already dead. Junior walked in and looked at his father. His eyes filled with tears his heart filled with sorrow. He let his emotions pour out. He cried and all I could do is watch. We all looked as the attendant closed the blinds. We all stood there caught up in our emotions. My thoughts like most of us standing there was revenge. I put my arm around my sisters shoulders and walked them out the room. I hadn't talk to my sisters in a few months. When we got upstairs Junior and Letha was holding on to their mother. I was talking to my sisters and Aunt Bea and Momma Cye were talking. They talked for a long time when we left we went back to the condo. Aunt Teeka, Aunt Bea and Momma Cye had to go to the funeral home to get the body sent back to Detroit. We had a chance to bond again just the five of us the next generation. We sat around listening to music and playing cards. Trying to take our mind off of what was going on around us. The four of us was playing spades and Letha was waiting her turn. She stood up.

"I'm tired. I have had my throat cut, tongue

cut out and left for deadand my daddy was killed. I want revenge. I want this to end before I have kids or one of you have kids and the cycle keeps going on."

"I'm with you cus, whatever we have to do. My mother got killed, my uncle got killed and I want this to end too." I said

"I'm in with you guys, I want this to be over but I want the person responsible for my father's death." Junior said with authority. This left the twins. Jada the aggressive one I knew would be down.

"I'm going back home. I don't like school and I want to be with my family." Jaden decided to finish her education. So when we left California she went back to school in Florida. She didn't want to even go to the funeral because she knew if she went home she wouldn't go back to school. She cried as she told everybody good bye at the airport. We all understood but her sister didn't want to leave her alone. Jaden left with Aunt Bea who took her back to school. They were just alike smart and knew what they wanted out of life. I watched them leaving the airport and wished I could be as dedicated and knew what I wanted out of life. We all left California with Uncle Mac's body. The long plane ride felt longer with the burden on what lies ahead. Aunt Teeka and Momma Cye were deep in their thoughts. When I looked in their faces I knew our lives wound change. I looked at all my siblings and cousins and told myself this next generation would end this war between the two families one way or the other.

Chapter 6

When we got back home we didn't even get a chance to get off the plane. The FBI was waiting as we exited the plane. They took Aunt Teeka down to talk to her. Momma Cye called her sister Aunt Bea put she was in Florida dropping Jaden off at school. They kept Aunt Teeka for four hours we all stayed with her to see what was going on. The FBI finally released her and she told us they had questions about her husband's death and also asked her if she knew he was involved with a California massacre in which seven police officer's were killed. Aunt Teeka looked worn out. Her husband's death, travel and the FBI had taken a toll on her. We all were looking forward to going home and relaxing. We picked up our cars from the airport parking lots and headed home. When we pulled up to the houses Aunt Teeka's door to her house was open. Momma Cye rode past her house and went straight to her garage next door at her house. I followed her in the garage with the car I was driving. She closed the door we all got out and followed Momma Cye to the basement cellar. She pushed a button and a door open. Both houses had this hidden cellar. Just like Aunt Teeka's cellar it had an arsenal in it. We all snatched gun's of the wall and ran out of the house. I told Momma Cye and Aunt Teeka that me and Junior would go in the front door and they wait at the back door. Letha and Jada would cover the side doors. Junior and I walked in the front door with our guns out. The house was turned upside down. We walked close to each other while looking for anybody in the house. We looked all over the first floor no one was there. Momma Cye and Aunt Teeka came through the back door with their guns out. When Aunt Teeka saw the way her house look she broke down. That was the first and only time I saw her lose it. Aunt Teeka fell to the ground tears streamed down her face as she called Uncle

Mac's name out. Her two kids ran to her side. Jada and I looked through the rest of the house. The whole house was turned upside down. I don't know what they were looking for but it didn't seem they found it. We walked back to the kitchen where Aunt Teeka, Momma and Junior were sitting at the kitchen table. They were reading the warrant that was left on the table.

Things really changed in the next few months after the funeral of Uncle Mac. Even at the funeral there were a lot of white men that we could tell were police or FBI. Every time Aunt Teeka left the house she thought she was being followed. She begin to be an recluse in her own house. Her problems escaladed when the Feds froze all her bank accounts and seized her house for tax evasion. Aunt Teeka had to live with us. They kept everything in the house to auction off. Luckily we had removed the arsenal the week of Uncle Mac's funeral. Aunt Teeka was only able to get personal things out the house before they locked it up. Momma Cye was Aunt Teeka's strength. They talked until the early morning hours. They cried together and talked about the men in their lives. I heard Momma Cye talk about my father the only man she ever loved.

She never said anything negative about him she only said he was a good father and a good provider. She told Aunt Teeka that she wish she had been more patient with him. Aunt Teeka talked about Uncle Mac openly. She said she had nothing but good memories of him and all the good times they shared. Sometimes all the kids would sit down and listen to the stories both ladies shared about their men and about how they always had each other's back. The mourning process was better with all of us together talking about the past and the good times. Everything cooled down a little after the house was sold. Momma Cye called us to a meeting with Aunt Teeka. She told us that the money she had in her accounts was gone. She said we had to have a plan to make it. She started crying and said she had hoped that her kids wouldn't have to go through the pain she suffered. Aunt Teeka went to her side and told us they had decided to do what they knew how, to take care of their family. I told Momma Cye that I wanted to get the money from my college fund. I knew I would never go. Junior also said he wanted to do that. Jada said she wasn't planning on finishing school and she wanted hers added to the kiddy. At first Momma Cye and Aunt Teeka was against it.

"We all are ready to have our families back like you beat it in our heads. Now you won't let us. I'm not going to college and I might die tomorrow, but I wouldn't care as long as I knew I had my families back." Letha lectured looking at her mother with tears in her eyes.

"I'm with Letha" I said and stood beside Letha. Jada and Junior stood up and stood beside us. It looked like a show down our parents on one side of the room we on the other. Letha and Jada had their hands on their hips. Junior and I with our arms folded looking strong and confident. We all stood their looking at our parents not moving a muscle. Momma Cye and Aunt Teeka looked at each other sternly then they both started laughing we all started laughing.

"We must be getting old" Aunt Teeka said.

"Ok kids have it your way, but we will run everything from the house and you guys do all the leg work.

Aunt Teeka and Momma Cye gave us a major connection and we used the money to buy large quantities of cocaine. We put it on the streets as Aunt Teeka and Momma Cye advised us. We set up four drug houses two on the Eastside and two on the Westside to package and distribute. TC -

NG was labeled on all our bags. Teeka Cye Next Generation was all of us together and everybody wanted to be down with us or they were against us. Soon we were moving product it most of the areas of Michigan. Junior and I recruited workers. Letha and Jada got small dealers to buy from us by giving them good deals. The product was good so the sale wasn't that hard. Aunt Teeka and Momma Cye stacked the money keep track of the drugs and distributed the money between us. All of us had our own money each week. We made more money than I thought was possible. We were in what I call the middle. Aunt Teeka and Momma Cye had dealers buying from us from their generation and we had all the younger generation. Our drug empire grew fast and furious within year. Aunt Teeka warned us there will be consequences. She made us always stay together.

Jada met a guy name Terrence. They started hanging out. Momma Cye was a little leery about him and had us keep Jada within our eye sight. One of us was always with them when they went somewhere. I know it put a strain on their relationship but they were in love. To my surprise this young man was very patient. One day he wanted to take Jada to the park. Letha said she would role with them. Junior and I had some business to take care of. Letha talked on her cell phone while Jada and Terrence walked ahead of her holding hands. An ice cream truck was stopped by some kids over by the swings in the park. Terrence asked Jada and Letha if they wanted some Ice cream. He walked over to the truck. Letha and Jada were talking about Terrance and hadn't notice the two guys approach them.

"Ah baby can I holla at you" one guy said as the other one approached Letha.

"I got a man" Jada responded and kept talking to Letha. Letha could smell trouble and held her purse tight in case she had to pull her gun out.

"I don't care about your man I just wanted to talk to you for a minute."

"She said she got a man, so why don't you guys keep pushing on" Letha said harshly.

"Bitch I didn't ask you" the guy said and back handed Letha. She fell to the ground and her purse went the other way. Then he pulled a gun out and told Jada

" give me your money and jewelry." When Jada turned around to see if Terrance was close the guy with the gun was hit with a two by four.

Terrence hit him again and again. The man's gun fell to the ground. The other guy tried to reach for his gun and Terrence swung his board and hit the man in the face. Both guys were on the ground as Terrence kept swinging his board. Letha picked up her purse and shot one of the guys. Terrence picked up the guys gun and he too shot the guy. Both men laid there bleeding and begging for their life's. Just a few minutes ago they were acting all hard with the women.

"We're going to let you go but don't fuck with my peoples again" Terrance told the men.

"Terrence that's not how we do things" Jada said as she took the gun from his hand. She shot one of the guys in the chest Letha shot the other guy in the head. Terrence didn't hesitate he took the gun from Jada and emptied it in both guys. "We never leave anyone so they can to come back at us" Jada told Terrance. He understood.

"Let's get out of here" he said. The park was empty by now and you could hear the sirens in the background. They walked calmly to Letha's car and drove away. Letha called a meeting when we got home. We always discuss issues with the family. Terrence became part of the family after that. He even spent nights at the house with Jada. Junior, Terrence and I ran a crew of twelve guys.

The three of us became cool like brothers. One day we went shopping at the mall. After dropping at least a couple thousand each we went to food court to eat. I spotted this fine red bone girl. She almost look like she was white but you could tell by her demeanor that she was black. I watched her from my seat. Junior and Terrence had their back to her and they couldn't see her. I tried to get her eye attention before I approached her. She kept looking my way while she got her food. I didn't get her eye contact but she look like she was interested. I looked at the table next to me and my good fortune was that it was empty. I thought she finally noticed me and smiled as she walked slowly towards our table. She was beautiful. Long black hair and a curvatious bottle glass figure. The body of a black girl but her features were like a white girl. The pearly white teeth mad her smile stand out. The dimples only accented her face. She was something you dream about. She approached the empty table and to my surprise she scooted over next to Terrence.

"Can I sit with you guys" Terrence looked up at her shook his head and kept eating. Junior jumped up.

"Sure, sit down" Dam I didn't expect this maybe she was feeling one of the other guys. I let my ego down as I tried not to stare at her. The situation was getting awkward for me no body was talking. Everybody was eating like her being there was a natural thing.

"I'm RJ this is my cousin Junior and this is Terrence" stumbled out my mouth. Terrence looked up from his plate and laughed and shook his head."

"I'm sorry guys, this is my sister, Marketta" Junior and I looked at each other. Then I looked at her gave her my sexist smile.

"I didn't know you had a sister, one as beautiful and down to earth as this" she smiled at me and held her hand out.

"Hi, Terrence has told me about you"

"Thank you brother" I said while slapping Terrence on the back. Junior couldn't believe he got looked over. He was the pretty boy of the group with his dads blue eyes and his fine yellow skin. But game wants game, and I sure wanted to get to know Marketta. After we ate Junior and Terrence walked around the mall while Marketta and I got to know each other better. She told me her father was white her and Terrence had different fathers. I enjoyed her company and when she said she had to leave I was a little disappointed. She made a phone call and told the

person where she was. I told her I'll catch up with her soon. She asked me to wait. I didn't want to meet her man so I walked away. She pulled me by the arm.
"I was just kidding you, I'm waiting on Terrence" She smiled and rubbed my arm tenderly.
"Girl why you playing with my emotions, you know I want you to be my baby mama" I said with a smile. Terrence and a jealous Junior walked up. She was smiling and looking at me so sexy.

"We can work on that, here is my cell number. Call me sometime." she pushed her card in my hand and kissed me on the cheek.

"Dam,RJ what you do to my sister? You got her cheesing like that."

"I don't know what I did but I'm going to continue doing it, holla at you later Marketta" She waved Terrence and her disappeared in the mall. Junior had a million questions but his bottom line was.

"She is fine as hell I don't know what see saw in you. She could have had this fine yellow brother here"

"But she wanted a real one" we slapped dap on each other and left the mall.

Chapter 7

Aunt Teeka called us all in for a meeting. Junior and I had our own crib and Letha had her own apartment in the same complex. Jada stayed with Letha most of the time but she still stayed at home. We all came to the meeting. Letha, Jada, Junior, Terrence and myself. She told us she had a bad feeling about today because her stomach was fluttering. Which usually means something bad was going to happen. She told us to stick together today and Momma Cye and she would be watching our backs. We had a big shipment coming in today. Ten kilos of pure cocaine was being delivered. We didn't trust anybody to handle that much product or that much money. The meeting took place in Monroe Michigan a white suburb. We rode up in couples. Letha and I, Jada and Terrence with Junior in the back sit. Aunt Teeka and Momma Cye were following us. We arrived at the office building about two in the afternoon. Letha and I got out and went inside. Junior, Jada and Terrance watched the front so that they could see if anybody else showed up unexpectedly. I rung the bell and was buzzed in. We walked in the first floor office where two Dominican guys were waiting.

"You look just like your mother" one of the guys said to Letha as he looked her over. She was in a business suit pumps and had a briefcase. I was dressed in an Armani suit with a tie. We both had on light bullet proof vest under our clothes that Aunt Teeka insisted we wear. We had bought from these guys before but never such a large quantity.

"What's up Sal"

"I'm cool brother" he said. "Let's get down to business. The other guy walked over to a closed door and opened it. I rest my hand on the small of my back and put it on my Beretta.

"Relax bro, he just getting the product."

"My bad Sal I'm a little over cautious." The other guy pulled out two duffle bags and put them on the desk. He stacked the ten kilos in bundles of five.

"Here is your product, where is the cash." I moved toward the dope and didn't notice Letha had slipped her gun out and had it by her side.

"You don't mine if I check things out"

"Go ahead son, knock yourself out." Letha walked over put the briefcase on the desk then walked to the opened door. She pulled her gun up as the other guy pulled an AK assault rifle from behind another desk.

"Hold on" Sal told his guy who was pointing his gun at Letha. Sal looked at me and my gun was pointed at him.

"Sal we just being cautious no disrespect" We all held our weapons up for battle until Letha came out the room. She lowered her gun.

"All clear in there cus"

"Sal we had to make sure we weren't being set up" Sal looked at me.

"I don't do business like that. Where's the money" Letha opened the suit case.

"This is two hundred thousand. My sister got the other seventy five in the car." Letha picked up her cell phone hit a number and told Jada to bring in the suitcase. Junior and Jada got out the car and walked up to the door. Sal's man walked to the front door and let them in.

"I will stay out here" Junior said he kept his eyes on his surroundings. Terrance was standing in front of the car with his semi automatic rifle. Sal's man came back in with Jada trailing him. Jada looked at Letha standing next to the drugs then at me next to Sal.

"We cool" I nodded to her. "Here is the rest" Jada put the suitcase and stacked the money on the table. Sal's man went over and started counting the stacks of money. There were in Five thousand dollar stacks so it was easy. When he finished he looked at Sal.

"Everything good on this in boss"

"Fine, I see you guys in a few months" Sal said as he got up ready to leave.

"Hold on a minute we're going to test each bag" Letha pulled her testing kit out the pocket off the briefcase. She looked at the small medicine bottles she had in a plaster sandwich bag. She pulled out some liquid and a dropper. She put five drops of the liquid in the bottle. She pulled a small knife out the bag. Cut the drug bag on the corner and put a little in the bottle. She shook the bottle while looking directly at Sal. When the color was darker then what she expected. She looked at me.

"This is some high quality stuff. Better than

we thought."

"I got another appointment in ten minutes. Are we through?"

"She's testing each bag, Sal. You got our money give us a minute." Jada went over to help Letha speed up the process. All the bags were good. I grabbed one duffle bag and Jada picked the other one up. Letha still had her gun to her side. We walked out the office and I saw Junior at the front door and I could see Terrance at the car. I then noticed two cars pull up. I hesitated then I thought about Sal saying he had another meeting. I looked back at Letha who took her other gun out for precaution. The guys in the two cars got out. They were all white. They looked at us and hesitated for a minute. One of them must have called Sal because they didn't move until he hung up the phone. Sal told them we were ok. We just kept walking. The six men walked pass us keeping their eyes on us as we kept our eyes on them. Jada and I was in front with the duffle bags on our arms and our guns in our other hand. Junior and Letha walked behind us looking over their shoulders as the men passed them. The last two guys passed us when Junior spun around and started shooting.

"They in the pictures, the pictures" all hell

broke out. One guy fell while the other one shot Junior in the leg. When he spun around he shot him in the back. Letha had two guns spitting bullets. The casings were jumping out her gun hitting the pavement one by one. The guys were caught in a cross fire. Aunt Teeka and Momma Cye was walking up to them from the side of the building pumping bullets in their bodies with two guns each. Sal and his man came out the office and started shooting at us. His only reason was they were white and we were black, he took their side. He thought he has in danger. I fell to the ground firing away. Jada got hit in the arm and yelled in pain. Momma Cye went to her side shooting emptying her two guns on the guy that shot her daughter. She asked her if she was hit. Jada said it was a flesh wound. Momma Cye's clip to her guns popped out and hit the ground. In one smooth motion she pulled two clips from her jacket and put them in the guns cocked them and continue shooting. For the next two minutes you heard a barrage of gun fire. I tried to lay low with the duffle bag in front of me then everything stopped. It was so quiet after so much fire power. The quiet after the storm. I looked up from the ground and saw a lot of smoke. Momma Cye picked me up and asked who shoot Junior. I thought it was a weird question at the time. But when I pointed to the guy on the ground she went over put a new clip in her gun and unloaded in the man's lifeless body. Then she picked up the gun he shot Junior with and put it in her waist. Aunt Teeka commanded.

"Get Junior in the car, he has been hit" I looked around for a split second to see Terrance run from the front of the office building. Sal and his man were laying against the front door of the office building. Their bodies punctured by bullets holes in their chest, face and legs. We lifted Junior to the car. We hurried because we heard siren's a distance away. We were in a secluded white area. We all got in our cars. We put the drugs and all the guns in the car with Jada and Letha and we let them leave first. Junior, Terrance and I pulled away next with Aunt Teeka and Momma Cye following. We had an exit plan and we drove deeper in the city. We drove to the section where a few blacks lived and pulled in a motel parking lot. Momma Cye and Aunt Teeka looked at Junior. He was hurt bad. Jada only had a flesh wound. We had to take Junior to the hospital. Aunt Teeka had us put Junior in the car with her. Momma Cye got in the back and worked on Junior. We started moving again going straight to the highway back to Detroit. Aunt Teeka called me on my cell while we were driving. She told me to go ahead and don't stop for nothing. She called Letha and told her the same thing. Momma Cye asked about Jada and Letha told her she was alright. We were almost to the highway when we heard the sirens getting closer. We all made sure we did the speed limit. I saw signs that the 94 expressway was one mile up. We were on a two lane road and the police cars pulled right up behind us. I didn't know what to do. Letha called me on my cell.

"RJ just keep driving. Don't let the police get in front of you." In my rear view mirror I saw the police cars flashing lights. There were three police cars. Aunt Teeka slowed down and started to pull over when the other police tried to get by. Aunt Teeka turned the car to the left and the police car ran into her. I watched in my rear view mirror as the police got out with their guns drawn. I didn't see Aunt Teeka or Momma Cye moving. I shook my head and called Letha.

"Did you see that? I hope everybody is alright."

"They will be fine. You know they always got our back." I could hear her sniffle before she hung up the phone. We hit 94 Expressway and made it back to our safe house. We pulled up together and Terrance jumped out to see if Jada was ok. He picked her up and carried her in the house. Even though it was a flesh wound she smiled and hugged her man tight. We were happy to be alive. That was our first real gun battle and everybody held their own. Letha decided that we should stay in the house until we heard from her mama Aunt Teeka. Letha and I went to do some small shopping so we could have food for a couple of days. She was in a bad mood. She was worried about her brother and mother. We all knew it would be a long night. I hugged my cousin for comfort and told her everything will be ok. Her cell phone rung it was Momma Cye. Letha put the phone on speaker and we just listened.

"Your brother has been shot. We are at the hospital in Monroe County. They are going to transfer him to Henry Ford Hospital in Detroit. You can meet us there"

"Is he alright? What happen to him"

"He was shot in a drive by."

"Where is my mama?"

"She is being questioned by the police. We had an accident while taken Junior to the hospital" Letha and I knew someone was around her. So she couldn't speak freely.

"They had a massacre up here and they are questioning us because Junior was shot."

"Who was killed?"

"I don't know but they said at least six or eight people was killed." She whispered put she also wanted the people around her to hear her. "I think they were white." I held the phone and said.

"Hi Mom we got this covered we will meet you at Henry Ford in a couple of hours. If there is any change call us."

"Alright son how is your sister doing?"

"She is fine she chilling with T"

"Tell mama and Junior I said I love them" Letha said with tears in her eyes. We hung up the phone and knew we didn't have much time to get rid of any evidence we had. Letha and I stopped by Home Depot on the way home. I got two shovels, four bags of cement, some plaster gloves and some large garbage bags. When we got back to the house Terrance any Jada were in the bathroom. I guess her arm wasn't too bad. It smelled like that had been having sex all over the house. When they came out the bathroom they both was smiling and grinning.

"Come on Terrence we got work to do" I took him to the back yard where I had backed the car up. The house had a privacy fence around the backyard eight feet high. We had it built so our neighbors wouldn't be in our business. I opened the truck of the car and got out the shovels. Terrence looked at me strange.

"Who we going to bury" I think he got a little nervous because he knew he was the outside one of the family. I saw his uncertainty.

"Fool this is for the guns. We can't use them again do you want those bodies on you?"

"Naw man, but truthfully I thought you was going to take me out"

"Boy quit playing you know you family and you prove it all the time bro" I gave him the black hand shake then a manly hug . "Let's get to work" we dug a hole four feet deep and four feet wide. I went and got all the guns out the car that Letha and Jada was driving. We took them in the house and we all put on gloves and wiped the guns totally off with a towel and degreaser. We open the garbage bags and put the guns in them. Terrence and I put on some new gloves while Jada flushed all our gloves down the toilet. We took the bags with the guns and dropped them in the hole we dug. I filled the hole with the four bags of cement. Terrance got the water hose and we filled the hole with water. After the water settled we filled the hole back with dirt and leveled it off. No one will ever find those guns unless they tear the house down. By them we will long gone and forgotten.

Chapter 8

Letha, Jada, Terrance and I went to Henry Ford Hospital. We met Momma Cye in the emergency room. The corridors where full of people lying in the hallway on gurneys.

"How is he doing?" Letha asked hugging her aunt.

"He's in surgery. It doesn't look good for him. He got shot in the back and they think he may have ruptured his spinal cord."

"Is he going to live" Letha couldn't hold back the tears.

"He's going to live but he may be paralyzed."

"Aw man that's not good" I couldn't believe it. My cousin paralyzed. I moaned with a heavy heart. Jada cried on Terrances shoulder.

"Where is Aunt Teeka?"

"She is still in Monroe they holding her for

questioning"

"They still questioning her from early today."

"Let's go outside and talk" Momma Cye led us out the side door to a bench. The four of us followed her. The area had grass with big trees and benches under the trees. Momma Cye walked to a bench far away from the others and sat down. Letha and Jada sat on her sides while Terrance and I stood up. She grabbed the girl's hands. Looked at me and asked "Did you talk care of the guns?"

"Yes, ma I did" she showed her thanks by a half smile then whispered so only we could hear her. "The police are holding Teeka because they feel she was involved in what went down at that office building." He all looked at her with tense anxiousness to hear the next words. "Because Junior had gunshot wounds and no evidence to his story of a drive by, they trying to connect them to the murders. They have Junior under police guard even while he is in surgery. The only way they can put Junior at the scene of the murders would be the bullets in his body. If any bullet matched the guns that were found at the scene then Junior and Teeka would be looking at some hard time.

"What you want us to do mama" Jada asked

squeezing her mother's had.

"I want you all to go home. Junior will be in surgery for about five hours. You need to take care of that package. Prep it and get in on the streets. We can't afford a lost. We are down to our last money. If there is any change in Junior I'll call you. Besides I don't want the police to get to know your faces. They will be watching Junior's room for a while. You guys stay together. Don't go anywhere alone." We all hugged each other and shed some tears. Everybody was teary eyed even Terrance. He was hurt because his girl was hurting.

We left the hospital stopped by our drug house and broke four of the kilos down. We broke them down to ounces. We took the rest of the drugs home to Gosse Pointe. We couldn't leave that much product in a drug house. Letha took control. She told all of us to get new guns from the cellar with silencers on them. We stashed the rest of the kilo's and took the ounces with us. We drove in two cars Terrence and Jada drove her SUV and Letha and I followed in a plain black chevy of mine. We went to each drug house unannounced. Letha and I always went in. Jada and Terrence watched our backs from the outside. We never wanted them to see all of us. That way if we needed one of us to spy on them we could. At the first house the crew opened the door and Letha and I walked in. Ray the manager of the house was glad to see us. He was a child hood friend that had started using drugs young. But had been working for us since we started and he was loyal. We dropped some ounces on him and told him how much money we expected back. We had so much product and the drugs was so good that everybody was able to break it down and make extra money. I told him I'll be back in one week and I expect to have my money and then he could re up for more. We repeated this process at the next two houses. When we arrived at the last house we were let in by Mike the manager. He looked at me before he opened the door and hesitated. Had I been thinking right and not thinking about my cousin Junior who usual goes with me I wound have sensed something was wrong. The door opened wider and I felt a gun in my ear.

"Keep moving and no one will get hurt" The voice said. I saw Letha reach for her gun. She was hit in the back by another man with the shot gun we left at the house for protection. It was Mike's partner Do-it. That was his name. He had been in jail for molesting a nine year old girl. He did ten hard years. While in jail they said the guys turned him out and called him 'Do-it' they made him 'do-it' and everybody. Letha looked up at me with those killer eyes. I looked at her and shook my head no. She knew that I meant it wasn't the right time. We had to catch them unexpectedly. Do-it looked at Letha. He had wanted her since he started working for Mike and had tried to approach Letha. But she turned him down and now he had the upper hand.

"Get up so I can search you"

"You don't want to search me, you want to feel on me" Letha said.

"Bitch if I wanted you I would have already had you"

"You could never have me" Letha retorted with a deadly look on her face. The other guy with the gun to my head told Do-it.

"Calm down and let's get this dope. You can have any bitch you want when you got the cash we going to make off this dope." I looked at Letha we knew somebody snitched on us. It had to be someone in one of the three houses we just left. They must have called ahead and told them we were carrying a large package. He pushed me over towards Letha and told Do-it to tie us up.

Do-it grabbed the large purse Letha was carrying. Looked in and saw all the dope. He pulled out the eight bags of pure cocaine eight ounces and stacked them on the table. His eyes got wider at that very moment he felt on top of the world. He thought he was in complete control and started spending his money in his mind.

"Search her then tie them up" his partner barked. He then took my two guns from my waist.

"Get up bitch" Do-it yelled. He reached out and snatched Letha by her blouse off the floor. Her silk blouse tore off exposing her very large breast. She wasn't wearing a bra. There were four guys in the house including me and everybody's eyes were on her full beautiful perky breast including me. They stood up nice and firm like they were saluting the president. I had to take my eyes off of them. I never knew my cousin was packing like that. Do-it started rubbing her body looking for her weapon. He found the 380 automatic in her back waist band. He felt her chest and started getting himself excited. He stood back looked her up and down then started massaging his dick.

"You want to search me or fuck me" Letha said in a sexual voice. I knew she had a plan.

"I want to fuck you" Do-it's dick was protruding out his pants.

"Do-it man just get the dope and let's role" his partner said as he gathered the drugs up and put them in a black bag he had in his pocket.

"I haven't been fucked in three years you sure you can handle this" Letha was sexually toying with him. I was ready to back her up.

"I CAN handle it" Do-it insisted.

"Let me see what you working with. You can fuck me right here. Let's see if you got the balls to pull it out and show me what you got." Letha rubbed her large breast then stuck one in her mouth. Getting all the guys aroused. Do-it unzipped his pants and pulled his pants down. Letha stared at his manhood. It was large not that I was looking.

"Dam baby, I don't know if I can handle that" Her voice was sexy. She got up and walked over to Do-it and stated playing with his dick. I never saw my cousin like this. The other guy was looking at her wishing he could fuck her too. She rubbed Do-it's dick it got harder. He grabbed Letha by the hair and put the gun to her head.

"Suck it bitch" Letha stared at him with a blank look. She was getting ready to put his dick it her mouth when. 'Bam, bam, bam.' There was a hard knock at the door. 'Bam, bam, bam' again Do-it pushed Letha back and went for the door. Letha reached to her ankle and pulled her other gun. No one saw what she did. She watched as the other man put the gun to my head and backed me against the wall. She put her gun to the side out of sight. She waited for the right time. At the door Do-it pushed Mike and told him to answer it. I heard the voice of a woman that was very loud. She said she had a thousand dollars to spend right now. Do-it's greedy ass told Mike to let her in. She walked in an assessed the situation before the door was closed behind her.

"I got two thousand dollars to spend" She pulled out a wad of money and threw it up in the air. All one hundred dollar bills floated around and around then fell softy to the floor.

"My man is a rapper he got plenty of money. I got to bring him some coke" The man holding the gun on me looked at the hundreds floating in the air and thought he was dreaming. With the dope and money he knew he would be living large for a long time. Do-it and Mike watched the money float slowly to the floor. The door burst open and Terrance came in shooting in the air. Letha sighted the man holding the gun on me aimed and let off three rounds before the man could gather his thoughts on what was going on. Jada turned and shot Do-it in the head point blank. His lifeless torso hit the floor and the rifle bounced to his side. Letha stood up and put her gun to Mike's head. Her tittes bouncing like basketballs as she hurriedly moved over to him.

"You set us up Mike, you was with them?" She didn't even care she was still half naked. She was ready to pull the trigger. She stopped when Mike said.

"I didn't do it but I think I know who did" Holding his hands up in a begging manner. Terrance hit him across his head with the butt of his gun. A knot sprung up on his head.

"Who set us up Mike" I asked as I retrieved my guns from the dead man's waist.

"Ray called Do-it and he went in the next room to talk to him"

"When did he call"

"He just called about an hour ago." We all looked at each other. Ray called Do-it after we dropped his package off. He knew we were on our way to Mike's spot. Letha didn't believe that Mike wasn't part of the plan. Two guys were dead in the room and we needed answers fast. Jada took off her jacket and gave it to Letha to put on. She saw Terrance staring at her breast. Letha kept her eyes on Mike and put the jacket on switching the gun to the other hand while putting her arms in the jacket. Her mind was racing she was thinking of a plan.

"Sit down Mike" Mike sat in the kitchen chair.

"Now you have to prove to us you weren't involved with this"

"What you want me to do? I'm telling the truth. I'll do anything."

"I want you to call Ray and tell him that Do-it left his share here. If you try to warn him I'll kill you. If he doesn't come I'll kill you. If I find out you are not involved I'll let you go." Letha said she pushed the gun to his temple hard. "We understand each other?"

"I'll call him but I have to tell you he asked me a month ago about sticking you guys up. I told him I didn't want any part of it." We all looked at each other. Aunt Teeka had already decided his fate even though she wasn't there.

"Just call him and put it on speaker." Mike picked up his phone and dialed Ray.

"What's up bro this Mike"

"What up man where is Do-it"

"He left with this guy. Did you get your package yet"

"Yea I got mine, I'm cutting and bagging"

"I ain't got mine yet I don't know what happen."

"They will properly hit you up tonight." Ray was getting ready to hang up

"A Ray, Do-it left something here for you. I don't know what's going on nor do I care. But he left 5 ounces of drugs here for you. You better come get this before my package comes. I don't want to be responsible for this shit in here. He said it was something you and him bought." Ray's mind raced. Do-it must have caught them outside he thought.

"How long ago did Do-it leave."

"He just left . He went to drop his boy off and he said he'll be right back. You coming to get this shit"

"Man I'll be there later" Ray tried to stall until he talked to Do-it.

"Man I don't know what you and Do-it did. But I'm leaving here in twenty minutes this shit will be left in this house and I aint responsible."

"OK man, I'll be there in fifteen don't leave."

"Ray you know I aint joking I'm out of here in twenty minutes."

"Alright I'm on my way" Ray hung up the phone and told his guys he will be right back. He gave instructions on what to do on his way out the door. Letha told Terrance and I to go move the cars. We moved the cars and came back inside. We then moved the bodies of Do-it and his accomplice to the back bedroom. Letha threw Terrance the shot gun and told him to pretend to be Mike's door man. Letha, Jada and I went into the next room. It was left of the kitchen. We stacked 5 ounces on the kitchen table so you could see them when you came in the house. Mike sat at the kitchen table so we could keep an eye on him.

"Mike you want to get high" I asked. He looked at me to see if I was serious. "What's your pleasure, you got ten minutes before Reggie gets here"

"I'll take a couple of toots of coke." Jada opened one of the bags and put a card full of drugs on a box. She took it over and gave it to Mike. He took the card made a few lines and snorted the white powder up his noise. The sensation he felt went straight to his head. It made him attempt to sneeze. He rubbed his nose took his finger and put it in the drugs then he put some in his mouth. He got an instant freeze his tongue got numb. He snorted a couple more lines then he sat back and smoked a cigarette. He was feeling good. Enjoying his high he almost forgot we were even there. A knock on the door brought him back to reality. Mike wiped his nose and went to answer the door. Ray pushed his way in. He glanced at Terrance.

"Who's that"

"That's my cousin from the hood I had to have someone watch my back."

"Where's my shit"

"It's in the kitchen, you better get that shit and get out of here. I don't want to have nothing to do with what you and Do-it is up to" Ray thought for a second 'why is he talking so much' but when he saw the drugs stacked on the table his thoughts went away.

"I'm getting ready to get paid. You should have been down Mike" Ray reached down to get the drugs and heard the click off three guns being cocked. He turned around just as Letha's bullet caught him in his shoulder blade. Jada's bullet caught him on his hand. He was trying to reach for his gun. I had no words for my child hood friend. He tried to plead with me with his eyes and body language I but two bullets in his chest. Letha and Jada scooped up the drugs and put them back in Letha's purse. Time wasn't on our side. We had been there too long. It was time to get out of there.

"I told you I wasn't involved" Mike said holding his hands up "You said you would let me go" We all looked at each other. Aunt Teeka's words came to our minds 'don't leave anyone to come back at you' Letha, Jada and I turned and let off a few rounds each from our guns without even thinking. Terrace walked over and unloaded one shot gun blast that silenced Mike's shimmering body. He didn't feel any pain. He had again got that ultimate high that one looks for after his first time. He never will feel any pain again. We loaded up and headed for Ray's dope house.

His guy let us in after noticing Letha and I. We all walked in the house casually.

"Where is Ray?" I asked talking to any of the three guys in the house.

"He went to make a run he said he will be back in twenty minutes"

"You know where he went" Letha probed.

"No I don't. What's with the questions?" The brave guy with the house rifle said. Letha and Jada standing next to him swung around with guns out. Letha put her gun to his chin.

"Nigger you work for us don't be getting it twisted." Terrance took the shot gun out his hand

and pushed him on the floor.

"I don't know where Ray went and I didn't know who you were. I was watching your house making sure someone don't come in here and stick us up. I don't know where Ray went but I wish he come on back to straighten this shit out." This big muscular guy was not backing down while showing respect for us. I started to put a bullet in his head. Letha walked over to him looked in his eyes put her 9 millimeter to his head. He looked straight at her not begging or flinching. Letha cocked her gun and pushed it on his forehead. She tried to force his head to move back. He pushed forward and stared into her eyes not blinking. We all waited anxiously. The man was ready to die. Jada had her gun on one guy and I had the other one covered. Terrance had Letha's back. Letha continued to push. You could see the imprint of the gun on the man's forehead. He still didn't blink or take his eyes off Letha. After a minute or so which seemed like hours Letha asked.

"You want a job running this house for us?"

"Yes I would Mam"

"What's your name"

"They call me Vapor"

"Vapor?"

"Yes, don't' fuck with the Vapor's" He said. We all just started laughing. Letha un cocked her gun and put it in her purse. Vapor's got up and she introduced us to him.

"This is Vapor's, he going to run this house for us. We waited for a half hour to see if anybody was wondering where Ray was. Nobody said anything else about Ray. We told Vapor's he was now in control of this house. The other guy that was second in command had a little attitude. But we felt Vapor would best protect our interest. We left after a while and went back to Grosse Pointe. We put up our arsenal and headed for the hospital to check on Junior.

Chapter 9

"Look Detective I have told you over and over again. I don't know anything about any office building or any white men that got killed there." Aunt Teeka pleaded.

"Mrs. Whitehead. This is your last chance. You need to take this plea and tell us what happen. If we find that the bullets in your son came from any of the guns picked up at the office building you and your son will be doing life in prison. You need to confess now. Your rap sheet wouldn't look good to a jury."

"I've told you I don't know what you talking about. I asked you for a lawyer and a phone call hours ago. When I get out of here I'm going to call the NAACP."

"The results will be back in ten minutes if you are innocent like you say then we will let you go.

But I suggest you sign these papers and write down your confession before this bites you in the ass."

"I've told you I don't know what you talking about." The Door open to the interrogation room and a tall white hillbilly looking man came in. He whispered in the detective's ear. They both got up and left. Thirty minutes later they came back in the interrogation room. They were smiling like they won the lottery.

"Your last chance Mrs. Whitehead the District Attorney is on her way. You need to sign this now" the Detectives were bluffing. The hillbilly looking cop had papers in his hand. They felt Aunt Teeka was involved but they didn't know how. A man burst through the door. He had a briefcase and court papers in his hand. He gave the detectives the papers.

"My name is James T. Wilson. I have a court order that you immediately release my client or I will be filing charges all the way to the supreme court for your unjustly treatment of my client. She has been in custody for six hours. She hasn't been charged or read her rights. She asked for a lawyer and you wouldn't allow her a phone call. This is the United States of America where people are innocent until proven guilty. Come on

Mrs. Whitehead" The lawyer helped Aunt Teeka out of the chair and led her towards the door. Aunt Teeka didn't say a word.

"Detective Worzinski and Detective Brown you will be hearing from me. If you have any more questions for my client you call me first. He gave them his card. "By the way please tell your chief I'll see him Saturday on the golf course." Aunt Teeka and her attorney walked out the station.

"Can I drop you somewhere?" he asked

"No thank you. When can I get my car back?"

"Your car will be released tomorrow and I'll have the case thrown out for lack of evidence. You won't have to appear here again. I'm CL Wilson's brother. I understand she had represented you before."

"Yes I'm sorry about what happed to her I saw it on television. Thanks for representing me." She asked the gentlemen if she could use his phone. She called Cye and found out about Junior and that everyone else was ok.
She gave James his phone back and asked him how much she owes him.

"Nothing, that was for my sister. Maybe we can have lunch sometime. I mean as attorney and client." He was trying to hit on Aunt Teeka.

Although she was aging she still kept herself looking good. Even when she was on a mission she looked like a will kept woman. She smiled at him she hadn't even thought of a man like that in years. But he did make her feel good. She liked that. She hadn't smiled like that in a while there was so much negativity in her life.

"On second thought could you drop me off at Henry Ford Hospital?"

"I'm heading to Detroit any way. I will be delighted Mrs. Whitehead."

"Please call me Teeka"

"And you call me James" On their way back to the city they talked a lot. James was an intelligent man. He had Aunt Teeka laughing and smiling so much that she temporally forgot her problems. They talked about everything. He told her Momma Cye had called Aunt Bea who got in touch with him. Aunt Teeka smiled as she thought about Cye's love for her. How she could call her sister to send a lawyer and the brother of the woman she killed after she had an affair with her husband that's true love. They pulled up at Henry Ford Hospital and Aunt Teeka got out and said thank you to James and told him to call her. Inside the hospital Momma Cye was waiting for Aunt Teeka . Junior had come out of surgery and the doctor's were ready to talk to her. We were all in a conference room waiting for Aunt Teeka . When she came in the two doctors' followed her. They told us that Junior made it out of surgery fine. They also said the bullet just missed his spinal cord. He could be paralyzed or after some time he might be able to walk with a limp. It was in God's hands. They couldn't be sure of the outcome it depends on his healing process. We all had a lot of questions for the doctors and they answered them all. The bottom line was Junior will be in the hospital for a while and he had to have rehabilitation therapy. The doctor's told us that Junior was under sedation until tomorrow and he told all of us to go home relax and he would see us in the morning.

We left the hospital and went back to Grosse Pointe. Momma Cye went in the kitchen and started cooking us something to eat. She loved to cook and would cook when things were on her mind. Aunt Teeka called us in the family room. Jada ran upstairs to take a shower. Terrance, Letha and I sat down to talk to Aunt Teeka. We told her about what happen at the houses. She told us we handled it right. She also told us we should really watch our back now because we are moving up and not only the crack heads and small time drug dealers, but the larger dope dealers will be trying to eliminate us the competition. We talked about our plans for the large shipment we got and about opening two more houses. She talked about everything but Junior. It was like she was avoiding talking about him. She asked Terrance about his family. I thought about his sister whom I have been too busy to call. Terrance said his mother was in a nursing home and his dad was dead. His mother told him he abandon her when she was pregnant. "What is your mother's name? Did she grow up Detroit? I might know her." Aunt Teeka asked him. Momma Cye came and told us the food was ready. We all washed our hands and sat at the table. Jada came downstairs and joined us. We all dug in we were hungry. When we finished eating we sat there full.

"Terrance you didn't answer my question"

"I'm sorry Ms. Teeka. My mother's name is Nicelle Henry she grew up on the West side. Do you know her?"

"The name sounds familiar."

"My mom didn't talk about my father just said he got killed when I was young."

"What was your father's name?" Aunt Teeka

kept probing.

"Terry was my father's name" Aunt Teeka dropped her glass she was drinking from. The glass hit the floor and wine spilled all over. Her stomach buzzed with butterflies.

"What? Did he have any sisters?"Aunt Teeka braced herself she already knew the answer.

"Yes my mother said he had one sister name Tanesha."

"Tanesha that's was my mother's name." I jumped and asked Aunt Teeka. "Could that be my mother he's talking about"

"I knew I saw you somewhere Terrance but you were little. Tanesha was my half sister and RJ's mother"

"So Terrance is really my cousin?" I couldn't believe it. No wonder he was so down with us. He really is family. Jada looked sad. She thought that Terrance was related to her and they would have to break up their love affair. Letha jumped on Terrance's back.

"You are my cousin too. I got much love for you Terrance."

Terrance looked at the look on Jada's face. He looked down to the ground.

"So the love of my life is my cousin too?" Momma Cye looked at Aunt Teeka. Their silence made Jada cry. Terrance put his hand on her shoulder" I'll always love you no matter what."

"You two are not related." Momma Cye said. Teeka and I are cousins through marriage of the game. Her father and my father were partners in the game. They both wanted boys put they got us. That's how we know so much about the game. They taught us the game at an early age. Our mothers instilled it in our minds. You two can keep fucking"

"Mama stop" Jada said blushing and rushing to Terrance open arms. That day we bonded like never before. Aunt Teeka and Momma Cye told us stories about both our fathers. Reggie my father was her partner in crime and Terry was her half brother she only knew for a short time. When she talked about Reggie Momma Cye left the room I saw tears in her eyes. I followed her out the room hugged her and told her I love her. Jada and Letha came in to comfort her. I went back in the living room where Aunt Teeka told Terrance and I a lot about our fathers. She told as about California and how my dad came to her and Momma Cye's rescue when their parents were killed. We stayed up until
day break talking and getting to know more about our new found family member. I knew from that

long talk Terrance and I would always be responsible for having our cousins back.

The next morning we got up had breakfast and went to see Junior. When we got there the doctor let us go in his room. Junior had tubes in his nose and arms. He couldn't move. He was sedated and in a full body cast. Aunt Teeka broke down she couldn't hold her feelings any more. Letha and Momma Cye took her out in the hall. She was hysterical I felt bad for Aunt Teeka. She had just lost her husband and now her son was lying in a hospital bed. Jada had tears in her eyes and I hugged her for comfort her. Junior didn't even know we were in the room. The doctors gathered us together and took us in a conference room. He asked Aunt Teeka if she was all right. Then he told us about Junior's progress. He said Junior had did well and was recovering good. But they didn't know if he would be able to walk again. The doctor said he had some feeling in his legs which was a good sign. They said all other signs were good. He told us that Junior would be able to notice us in a couple hours. He told us to come back in three hours. We all left the hospital and Terrance and I went to check on our money. Letha and Jada took their mother's home to spend some time with them. We collected money from two of the houses. But when we got to the last house they came up short and Vapor was missing. Tim the guy who use to be with Ray was in the house. He said Vapor left with fifteen thousand that we had made. Terrance and I didn't buy it. We drew our guns and the guy holding the shot gun pointed the shot gun at us. Tim pulled his gun and we were caught in the middle. Tim started talking "I told you Vapor left with the money."

"So why you draw your gun if you not guilty?"

"I know what happen to Ray. I'm just protecting myself."

"So where you going to work now" Terrance asked. Tim kept his gun out but had second thoughts about fucking with us. He didn't have enough heart. Terrance turned to the guy with the shot gun

"You're on his side"

"No I work for you he told me to do this." Terrance turned around and pulled the trigger of his 45 millimeter hand gun. He hit Tim twice in his chest. He fell to the ground clutching his chest. Both of us spun around and had our guns on the guy with the rifle. He would not have had a chance to left it and fire on us. I put the gun to his head.

"What happen to our money" he wanted to live he didn't try to be hard like most men when they know they are getting ready to die.

"He killed Vapor and put him in the trunk of his car. He gave me two thousand" he reached in his pocket and gave Terrance the money. "I didn't have anything to do with it." Terrance and I looked at each other. We knew we should kill him but our crew was getting small and we needed him to watch this house and get other crew.

"If I let you live you are going to owe me. I want you to be loyal and dedicated to me."

"I can do that I promise man, I'll be loyal to you." The man proved his loyalty and told us where Tim hid the money. Terrance gave him the two thousand back and told him he wanted this house up and running today. He also told him to get rid of Tim's body. We were taking a chance trusting him but at some point you have to try to trust somebody.

We took the money back to the house and had lunch with the other family members. Jada and Terrance were up in the room when the phone rang. It was the doctors from the hospital. The door bell also rung when I answered the phone and Letha answered the door. Two detectives entered the house. They wanted to talk to Teeka Whitehead. Letha led the detectives in the kitchen where we were eating. The doctor's were on the phone and told me that they needed us down to the hospital immediately. He would not say why but he said he needed us at the hospital as soon as possible. I hung up the phone and looked at the police then at Aunt Teeka. She was holding her stomach before the police said a word. Momma Cye held her hand as the police told us Junior was dead. Letha screamed so loud and hard that Terrance came down stairs with his gun out. He saw the police and put it up. Jada, Letha, Aunt Teeka and Momma Cye huddled together and cried profusely. Tears flowed down my face I couldn't believe Junior was dead. I asked the police what happen. They waited patiently until everybody was listening. We all held hands and Momma Cye said a prayed for Junior. We were silent for a minute while we mourned him together. We thought he had died from complications from his surgery. The detective finally had something to say. He spoke up.

"Mrs. Teeka Love Whitehead your son Mac Arhtur Whitehead Jr. died at Henry Ford

Hospital today at 2:30 PM." We all held our breath waiting for the cause of death. Aunt Teeka shook her head no she didn't want to believe it.

"He died from two bullet wounds in his head from someone using a 9 millimeter with a silencer."

"What? No that can't be true we just left the hospital an hour ago." A crying Momma Cye said.

"I'm sorry Miss someone snuck in his room and killed him" Aunt Teeka fainted. I called 911. The police called on his walkie talkie and the ambulance was there in two minutes. They rushed Aunt Teeka to the ambulance and Momma Cye and Letha went in the ambulance with her. Jada, Terrance and I followed the ambulance to the hospital with the detectives giving us a police escort. My heart went out to Aunt Teeka and Letha to lose two family members within months. When we arrived at the hospital Aunt Bea and James L. Wilson were talking to the administrators of the hospital. Aunt Bea wanted answers. Why her nephew was dead in a hospital with tight security. She told them law suits will follow. I never saw Aunt Bea lose her cool. Today she lost it. She had stayed in the background and true to the justice system only to see her family murdered and slain. No one ever paid for their deaths and she felt the justice system failed her. The years of education and years of being an attorney and judge had her doubtful she was on the right side. Her nephew was in the basement on a slab in the morgue. Her sister Aunt Teeka has lost her will to live and is lying in a bed on the brink of insanity. A pastor came in the meeting room along with the doctors. We waited for Momma Cye and Letha. The doctor's admitted Aunt Teeka to the hospital upstairs and they were on their way down. When they arrived the pastor prayed for us and we again held hands and let all our emotions surface. Aunt Bea, Momma Cye, Letha, Jada, Terrance and I shed our tears for our brother, cousin, nephew and friend. After the pastor left the doctors came in with the police detectives that came to the house. After giving their condolences they told us they have to ask us some questions. Then they would answer ours. The detectives asked us if we had any enemies. They told us that Junior was killed by what they thought was a mob style hit. Two bullets to the head and one in the chest to the heart someone wanted him dead. The detective questioned us for twenty minutes until Aunt Bea had enough. She told them that her family needed time to mourn. If they had any more questions contact her office. She gave them her card. The detective's left and we all got in the elevator and went upstairs to see Aunt Teeka. She was in a room with James at her bedside. We all pilled in her room. Aunt Teeka looked so peaceful to me. She looked like she didn't have a care in the world. After our visit with Aunt Teeka we set up time frames and agreed that someone would always be by her side until she got out the hospital. James Wilson agreed to stay with Aunt Teeka until someone came back. That gave us a chance to make arrangements for Junior's funeral. Aunt Bea wanted all of us to come over her house. She had something she wanted to show us. Aunt Bea's house was fabulous. She lived in a mansion. I had never been in a house so nice. She showed as around. Letha and Jada went upstairs and when we got upstairs after being showed the rest of the house, they were in Letha's old bedroom looking through her stuff. Everybody was trying to keep their minds off Junior. Aunt Bea called us to her movie room. She had all of us sit down while she told us about her last twenty years of findings. She first told us that neither Aunt Teeka or Momma Cye knew about what she was doing. She explained after her mother and father was killed she hired a private detective to find out what happen in California since the police closed the case and gave Mark Gucci only three years. She pushed a button and a projector came from behind a wall. She told us that some of these pictures may be a little graphic put she felt that we all must get to the bottom of this. Not only for our generation but also for the next generation that will follow us. She showed us pictures of her parents. Her father in a chair with a bullet in his head his eye lids were taped open to watch his wife being raped. Her mother on a bed tied down blood running down her legs her throat slashed from ear to ear. Aunt Teeka's mother was sitting in a pool of blood. Gun in hand and bullet hole in her head. The pictures were so gross. We had been told the stories but until I saw the pictures I didn't know how deeply hurt I would be. I looked at Letha, Jada and Momma Cye. They all had tears in their eyes and revenge in their hearts. She went on and told us how Letha was found in a bath tub blue and unconscious with duck tape on her lrgs, arms and mouth. Aunt Bea said she thinks Aunt Lolo Teeka's mother put the tape over Letha's mouth and legs so she wouldn't move or make a sound. She really saved her life. Letha had blocked her memories of that horrible day. Now she remembered it was her Grandma who told her to get in the bathroom and be quiet. She told her she was playing a game and told her not to move. She showed us pictures of Aunt Teeka and Momma Cye in mental hospitals. She continued with my dad Reggie and Uncle Mac coming to California to help his cousins ex. Letha's father was my dad's cousin. She had pictures of the shoot out at each one of the Gucci houses. She showed us pictures of everything that has happened between the two families for the last twenty years the deaths the killings and the slaughters. Aunt Bea said that she was trying to do things according to the law. But now she feels the law and the justice system has betrayed her. She said she could no longer stand by and watch her family murdered. She pushed a button and had a picture of the Gucci family tree. See had deceased on the ones that died. It started from their Mother and Father down to the next generation that would be our age. She even had addresses and the type of business they were in. James Gucci, Leon Gucci, Tom Gucci and George Gucci III were pictured walking with other people and known to be in Michigan a lot. Aunt Bea said that there were three girls but they weren't in the business. They're family shipped them out of the country. She said she wanted us to work together and use all the resources she had and the system has. We left there and went to the funeral home to make arrangements for Junior's funeral. We left crying and with heavy hearts. To see our family our blood in those pictures stuck deep in our minds we all had a chip on our shoulders. We now didn't care about building our drugs empire our or the money that came with it or anything else but getting even with the Gucci's.

Chapter 10

Junior's funeral was sad. Aunt Teeka cried the whole time. Momma Cye sat on one side of her and Aunt Bea on the other. They felt her pain. The whole church was sniffling and crying. Letha sat stoned face and she didn't shed a tear her eyes were clued on her brother's casket. I tried to think picture her thoughts. I comforted her by putting my arm around her shoulders. She laid her head on my shoulder with her eyes still on the casket. I could feel the shivers in her body as she fought back the tears. Terrance was holding Jada wiping away her tears with a napkin. Her chest heaving up and down she fell over on Terrance's legs. Her screams and cries could be heard throughout the church. Anyone who knew her or anyone in the family had tears in their eyes.

The people flowed by the casket paying their last respects. They stopped at Aunt Teeka hugged her and gave their condolences. Big time players in the game told Aunt Teeka that they would have her back in whatever she wanted to do. It looked like a community was coming together tired of the killings of the young people. But only the family knew the war has just begun. When the service began and the ushers closed the casket Letha jumped out of my arms went to the casket. "No I want to go with my brother, no she screamed." Terrance and I went to help her along with the church ladies in the growd. Aunt Teeka started beating her knees yelling

"Not my baby, not my baby why my baby?" Screams were coming from the back of the church. It was chaotic. People were in the isles when someone burst through the crowd running and screaming. I could not see a figure because I was on the end seat holding Letha. My heart skipped a beat I thought the worst. I had my gun on me just in case and I saw Letha's in her purse when I got her some tissue. I didn't want anything to go down at Junior's funeral. I was always thinking about protecting the family. I reached for my 380 automatic just as the figure reached where I was sitting. I saw a female image pass me going towards Aunt Teeka

"Mama I'm sorry, Aunt Teeka I'm sorry" It was Jaden. She ran up to Aunt Teeka and put her head on her lap. "I'm sorry Aunt, I'm sorry" Aunt Teeka rubbed her hair and she stayed on the floor hugging her legs and crying. Momma Cye cried and tried to comfort her daughter also. Her twin sister Jada went to her side and sat there with her crying their hearts out as their mother held them. They wouldn't let go of Aunt Teeka. The pastor walked up to the podium with a handkerchief it his hands tapping his eyes stopping the tears from running down his cheeks. He talked with emotion in his heart trying to keep his composure. He cleared his trembling voice and choose his words wisely then said

"This family is grieving a community is grieving" he looked at Aunt Bea and she gave him the cut it sign with her hand under her neck. "There are no more words to say. Please pray for this family. The celebration of the young life of Mac Arthur Whitehead Jr. is over. Funeral directors please come forward." We were glad it was over. I waited patiently until the family members seated on my roll passé. I joined them going down the aisles following the casket. Aunt Bea was holding Aunt Teeka up with Momma

Cye on her other side. Jada was with Terrance and Letha and Jaden walked together holding each other up. I let them pass and started walking by myself when someone hugged me tight held my hand and walked with me. It was Marketta Terrance's sister. She looked in my eyes and softly whispered in my ear

"I will always be there for you if you let me. I will never let you be alone" those words coming from her made me feel better. I've been so busy with family business I haven't had time to get to know her. All that would change now. I would somehow make the time. She held on to me and I walked down the aisle with my head up. I didn't want any one there to think for no reason I was weak. Even though I was in pain and hurting I was proud to have a beautiful stallion on my arms to comfort me. I could see all the guys looking at me with animosity and jealousy.

After we left the cemetery the limo's took us home. I rode with Marketta in her car. She took a detour. Told me she had to change clothes put on something more casual. I didn't mind I needed a break to think. I kept seeing Junior laying in that casket and the rest of the family mourning. My heart was hurting inside. It hurt me that there was nothing I could do to make anyone feel better. When we got to her house I sat on the plush couch while she went to change her clothes. My mind again drifted off to Junior and all we been through. He was really like my little brother and I felt responsible for what happen to him. I felt I didn't protect him like I should. The tears finally steamed down my face. After a few minutes my tears turned to sobs and my sobs turned to a full cry. I couldn't stop. I let it all out. When I rose my head up I had a shoulder that I was crying on. Marketta was holding me tight wiping my tears away with tissue. I let out all my sorrow. I felt embarrassed and I apologized to Marketta holding my head down. She held my face lifted it up and told me that I should never apologize for showing my emotions. I hugged her and put my head on her shoulders. I notice through my tears that she wasn't wearing a blouse. My head rested on her breast and my tears dripped on her smooth skin. She raised my head looked at me and kissed me deeply. Her mouth was warm and tantalizing. Her tongue was soft as cotton. She caught me by surprise and I wasn't ready for what she wanted from me. She soon changed my mind. Her tongue kissed the tears from my face. Then she kissed me passionately for a few minutes. She put her hand under my shirt and played with my nipples. Her hard breathing was making me relax. She tenderly kissed my eyes then she pushed me back on the couch. She got on top of me and unbuttons my shirt. I faded into the fantasy. A beautiful woman with white features light skinned with long black hair and aggressive. Not scared to show her freaky side. I felt her warm lips on my chest. She kissed my chest tenderly. Then she made small bites on my sides. It felt good. I laid back and closed my eyes falling deeper into her folic of love. With the small pain I felt with her bites I didn't feel her un zip my pants. Her hands rubbed my manhood softly and made it cater to her wants. She slid her tongue in my naval and licked in and around it. She looked into my eyes and licked from my naval down to my pubic hairs. Gentle pulling my hairs her mouth enclosed my dick. She looked at me as she engulfed all my nine inches. Slowly she rose up and down pulling my pubic hairs softly. The pain and pleasure at the same time had my body asking for more. Her tongue licked the shaft of my dick. Up and down on the side. She was taken her time relaxing my mind and body. She let my body simmer down while she pulled off my pants and under pants.

She kissed my knee caps and did more work on my dick. When it was hard enough she put it under her slip. I didn't notice she only had on a slip. The warmness inside her pussy swallowed me with delight. She moved slow and methodically. I wanted to call out her name. My state of mind weak from today's activity I taught about Junior. I pictured him in the room smiling saying it should have been him. My body couldn't take the good love she was putting on me. I ejected my juices inside her. She did not stop riding me. She put her head on my chest held me with her arms and rode me until my dick again rose to the occasioned. She held me tight and pumped up and down slowly until I again filled her body with a squirt of the succulent juices from my satisfied body. We laid there and I drifted to submission.

Marketta got off of me and pulled my arm to take a shower with her. After the shower she ironed my wrinkle clothes and we headed towards the house. Marketta talked a lot and I listened. When we arrived at the house I introduced her to the family and friends that were still lingering around from the funeral. Aunt Teeka, Aunt Bea and Momma Cye were talking in the living room.

Momma Cye called me over.

"You alright son" she asked my and hugged me.

"I'm ok Momma Cye. Where is Terrance upstairs?"

"He went to the store. The girls are up stairs."

"He went to the store by himself. You let him go?"

"He went with one of the guys who was at the funeral."

I took Marketta upstairs and introduced her to the girls. They bounded right away. She was a people person and she could get along with everybody. The girls loved her so they put me out the room. I went down in the cellar to get my weapons. I told myself I will never go anywhere without my wallet and my gun again.

The long day was finally over and the thoughts of my cousin Junior laying in that casket haunted me. I would wake up in the middle of the night with cold sweats. The days turned into nights that turned into months and I still woke up in a sweat. It was as if Junior was telling me to find the people responsible for his death. I never mentioned this to anyone. In fact the only one that knew about my dreams was Marketta. She held me when I woke up until I feel off back to sleep in her arms. Marketta got close with all the girls. Jada because she was dating her brother and Jaden tranfered back home and enrolled at Wayne State where Marketta went to school at. Letha was like their big sister they shopped, talked and hung out together. Terrance and I kept our business moving. But our motivation wasn't all the way in it. One afternoon we were going to check on one of our drug house. I told Terrance about the dreams and how I would picture Junior in the casket. Then I'd wake up sweating. He looked at me.

"For real RJ you are having dreams about Junior too."

"Why are you having dreams" I thought I was by myself having dreams about Junior. He told me that Jada did. "Jada has the same dreams at night. I have to hold her to stop her from crying." He told me that Jada told Letha and she too was having bad dreams about Junior. So much that she had to go stay with her mother. I couldn't believe that all of us were having dreams about Junior. I went got back home after collecting money and issuing some more drugs to the houses. I talked to Aunt Teeka and Momma Cye. They told me that Junior's soul couldn't rest in peace. That we couldn't rest either until his killer paid for taking his life. Terrance and I listened in disbelief. Jada and Letha were also awed when they heard this. We had to come up with a plan to find the killers of our cousin and brother.

Chapter 11

Little did we know that in Bloomfield a suburb on Michigan, the Gucci's next generation had gathered for a meeting. They were discussing the progress of finding the killers that massacred their family. Leon, George III, James and Tom Gucci were there with their henchmen. Two of their cousins were killed a few weeks ago and they wanted to find the ones responsible. They had no leads but had giving money in the streets and paid informants to give them information. The streets weren't talking to white guys about a black family. Leon spoke up. He told them that his sister Dena was working on a connection and we should have some valuable information in a few days. They were migrating from California and trying to take over the Westside drug market. They had policeman and judges on their payroll. So they knew it was only a matter of time before they found the people they were looking for.

Dena couldn't wait to call her friend she met in college in California. She told her she would call her when she got in Michigan. She picked up her cell phone.

"Hey girl how you doing? I just got in town."

"I'm glad you called I'm dying to see you I missed you so much" Jaden smiled at the sound of her voice.

"You couldn't have missed me as much as I missed you" Dena said and Jaden could feel her smiling through the phone. " I'm in Bloomfield but you can meet me in Farmington at my uncle's old house. No one is there and you can show me how much you missed me." Jaden blushed at the thought of her secret lover. Dena gave her an address. She wrote it down on her notebook and hung up the phone.

"Who had you smiling like that?" her twin sister asked her. Jaden pondered her answer. She had wanted to tell her sister that she was gay but didn't know how. She felt the time was right since she knew her sister could obvious see the glow in her face Jaden looked at her twin nervously and said.

"Jada I have something to tell you. I have been trying to tell you this for a long time but I didn't know how."

"Sis you know you can talk to me about anything"

"Jada I'm gay. I like women. I've never even had a man." Jada swallowed hard and looked at her sister.

"How you going to be gay? I'm not. Where did that come from.?" Jada didn't want to accept that her sister liked woman. She thought back and remembered how she looked at the other girls when they undressed in front of them. She never saw her with a boy of a man. But she thought Junior was fucking her like he was Jada when they were young. Jada had so many questions and her sister answered them as best she could. Jaden asked Jada not to tell the family. She said she would tell them when the time was right. Jaden talked about how she met her new love at school. She told Jaden she made her feel alive and free. She didn't care who saw them together. She just loved being with her. She told Jada explicit details about their sexual desires. Jada almost threw up. She couldn't phantom her being with another woman. Her twin sister is gay. That would have to get some getting use to. Jada knew it wasn't hereditary. She was strictly dickly. The twins met Letha and Marketta for dinner at Oakland Mall. They ate and the other girls notice how she was smiling and engaging in their conversations. She looked so happy she was in love. Letha noticed the good mood she was in and called her out.

"Jaden why are you giggling so much you had some dick?"

Jada looked at her sister waiting on her response. Letha and Marketta waited. "You got a man you haven't told us about." Letha probed on.

Jaden looked at her sister for advice. Jada's eyes told her sister to tell them. Jaden looked at her girls and lowered her head.

"I've met someone I like but it's not a man it's a woman."

"A woman" Letha said. It didn't sink in well. You like women?"

"I'm attracted to woman and I have been gay most of my life. I've always looked at women. I never had a man touch me."

"What I can't believe that. I saw my brother creeping from your house a lot early in the mornings. I thought he was doing both of you girls."

"It was me he was seeing" Jada spoke up. Always protecting her sister at all cost. "I'm fine with her being gay. I love you unconditionally. Jaden, nothing can stop that and never will." Jada got up and kissed her sister on the cheek and hugged her. Letha grabbed her cousin's hand and told her she loved her. She told her she will just have to accept her sexuality. Marketta told us that her close cousin was bi sexual. She said she couldn't decide who she wanted a men a woman. That eased the tension and everybody laughed. They all had a little wine and talked for a while. Jaden's phone rang. She told the person on the other end she was on her way. She told her sister she needed to borrow her car. Jada gave her the keys. She hugged everyone kissed her sister and held her hand.

"Thank you for being so understanding. You made that easy"

"I will do anything for you and I'll always have your back."

"Love you sister" Jaden said. She walked away from them hurrying along to meet her secret lover. Jada rode with Letha back to her apartment. Marketta went to her house to make sure I had something to eat when I came home. Terrance and I were waiting at Momma Cye's house. We needed them to back us up we had a minor problem at one of the houses. We got our guns and vests on and went out the house. We didn't know that Aunt Teeka and Momma Cye were weaponed up and right behind us.

We arrived at the west side house. Letha and I went in first. We found out that some white boys had come over with a junkie. They let him in and the white man killed the man holding the shotgun before he let his other guys in. They took ounces of drugs we had and flushed the bagged drugs with 'TC-NG' on them down the toilet. They left their drugs and told the house manager that if he wanted to sell drugs on the Westside that he had to sell their drugs. Letha was furious. She looked at the house manager.

"How the fuck you going to let someone come in and take your drugs from you" She looked at the man and walked pass him to the kitchen. I opened the door for Jada and Terrance. Terrance kept a look out and Jada went in the kitchen with Letha. They talked and looked in the cabinet. I had my gun on the manger as I was questioning him. I asked him how many guys were there and who let them in. The girls came back from the kitchen. Letha had some lighter fluid in her hand and Jada had a picture of water. Letha walked up to the man who was seated and squirted the lighter fluid on his feet.

"Dam what I do" The frighten man asked. Letha didn't hesitate she struck a match and flung it towards his feet. The flame went out before it hit his feet. "You crazy what you want what I do?" Letha struck two matches together. Looked in his face and dropped the match. The flame ignited his shoes caught on fire and he tried to stop it out. Letha threw some water on his feet and the flame went out. The man screamed in pain. The flame had just begun to reach his feet through his shoes. His feet was smoking. Letha got in the man's face.

"Were the men that came here White or Black" the man shouted they were white. Jada picked up the lighter fluid and put poured it on his feet and on his legs up to his knees. Letha struck the match again

"When they coming back to pick up their money"

"They said they would be back in three days and we better have their money. They also said that if we told anybody they would kill us." The man watched the flame in Letha's hand. The matches were almost burning her fingers. She looked at the flame and dropped the match. The man screamed in terror. Terrance picked out the window and saw a cop car pull up. Letha's and my phone rang simultaneous. I looked at her then my caller ID. It was Momma Cye all she said is you got company. Aunt Teeka told Letha the same thing. Jada poured the water over the man's legs. His pants and shoes were smoking. Letha stuck her gun in his mouth and said.

"You better not say a word." Terrance and I put him in the bathroom tub and locked the door. Jada pulled Terrance to the couch and snuggled up next to him. She put both their guns between then. Just in case they needed to reach them. Letha pushed me down in a kitchen chair and sat on my lap. She opened her blouse and put my hand on her chest. Everything happened so fast I didn't know what they were doing. The front door was kicked open and the two policemen walked in with their guns out. The girls screamed. They saw us coupled up. Then I heard a familiar voice behind them.

"Officer's I called you. Thank you of coming my daughters are in there they are only fourteen and fifteen." Momma Cye walked over to Jada snatched her arm. Get your ass in that car your daddy going to kill you. Letha removed my hand and buttoned her blouse back up.

"What the hell you waiting on an invitation? I

know I didn't see his hand in your blouse. Your fast ass is in for an ass kicking. Get your ass out of here." Letha jumped up and left through the front door. The two white men were confused. They thought they were raiding a drug house. They were going to take the money and drugs and give them back to the Gucci's.

"Thank you officer are you going to arrest these boys."

Momma Cye was pouring it on a little thick for me. Terrance looked at her then looked at the guns between his legs. He knew he would pull out the gun instead of going to jail. He started sweating. "Arrest them" Momma Cye said again. The men looked at each other then walked out the door. Momma Cye followed them to their car. She was complaining all the way. She said she wanted us arrested and wanted to see their badges to get the numbers to make a complaint. The men got in their car and drove off. Momma Cye got in the car with Aunt Teeka, Jada and Letha and drove away from the house following the police car down the road. After a couple of blocks Momma Cye turned around. When they returned to the house Terrance had gotten the guy out the bathroom. The guy saw Aunt Teeka and started begging for his life. He was an old schooler and he knew Aunt Teeka and feared her. She looked at Terrance and I then she said we need to talk. Jada picked up her gun from the couch. She shot the man twice in the head. Terrance and I took the body through the alley and put it in a garage a few doors down. When we came back we fixed the front door. Then we had to face Aunt Teeka and Momma Cye. I knew they were mad. They told us to be careful in whatever we do. She was more upset that we didn't plan ahead. She told us that we should always have an escape route. Momma Cye asked us our next move. Letha told her about what the house manager said. I told her that Terrance and I would stay there the next few days twenty four seven. We were ready to invest the time to wait on who ever came back. Aunt Teeka told us that the only reason that we were having so many problems is because we didn't have a loyal crew. The ones we had always turned on us Terrance chimed in.

"That means you tried to make all the money and you didn't share your wealth with your crew. You can't keep your crew happy if they see you making all the money and they don't see a future for them shelves." We were being scolded by our parents and yelled at by our partners. Momma

Cye broke her silence and uttered.

"We are not here to make you guys feel bad. We just want you to survive in a deadly game. Teeka and I have lived our lives. Some good times some bad. Now we decided to live the rest of our lives protecting you guys. We don't want some one's bullets cutting your life out without us being there with you to die for or to save you." Momma Cye had a tear in her eye. She told Jada and Terrance to go the store with her. They returned with blankets, pillows, food and games. It looks like we will be staying together for the next few days. Letha and Aunt Teeka set up the beds and Momma Cye put a schedule together.

Momma Cye had been trying to reach her daughter for a while. She asked Jada did she know where her sister was or was going.

"She borrowed my car and went to see a friend here from school. She told me she would be back later tonight." Momma Cye didn't say anything but she was worried. Usually when she called her daughter she would call her back. Aunt Teeka and Momma Cye cooked up the drugs left at the house by the white guys. We let them set and later Terrance and I cut them up. Jada and Letha bagged them. Customers started to come by after a while. When the word got out that we were giving large rocks the crack heads started coming. The traffic was coming fast. We hung in there. The next thing we knew it was morning. Momma Cye dialed her daughter's number and still didn't get a response. She woke Jada up and asked her if she heard from her. Jada tried dialing her sister from her cell. Jaden didn't answer. Her mother questioned her about where she went. Jada started getting nervous.

"Who did she go see? Have you ever met this person"

"No mama she was a friend that she met in Florida. They went to the same school."

"A girl and she stay's overnight without calling someone" Momma Cye was almost in tears. She couldn't explain why. But all parents know when something is wrong with their kids. Letha was sleeping in the room with Jada she woke up and listened to what they were saying.

"Mama did you know Jaden was gay. She likes women."

"Of course I knew I'm not stupid I see what's going on she never brought any guys around."

"She said she was meeting her friend and she was happy and all excited to meet her."

"Did you even ask what her name was?" Jada lowered her head. She tried to think while she dialed her sister's cell again. No answer. She started crying. Aunt Teeka, Terrance and I ran into the room with our guns out. We were half sleep we had just layed down a couple of hours ago. Momma Cye told us that she thought something was wrong with Jaden. She hadn't been able to reach her and had a feeling something was wrong.

Chapter 12

When Jaden arrived at the house in Farmington Dena was already there. She opened the door when she saw Jaden get out the car. Dena was happy to be with her friend but sad because she knew what lies ahead. She greeted her friend with an extra long hug. She kissed her and Jaden stuck her tongue deep in her throat. That always turned Dena on. She liked the way her small tongue invaded her mouth. She got moist between her legs and invited Jaden in the bedroom. Jaden didn't look around she trusted her friend with her life. Dena kissed Jaden and begin taking off her clothes. Jaden kicked her shoes off and Dena took her blouse and pulled it over her head. She sucked on her breast and took her pants and panties off. Jaden stood before her completely naked. Dena looked at her lustfully and pushed her on the end of the bed. Her legs dangled off the end of the bed. Dena got her knees and started licking her pussy. She stuck her tongue inside and watched Jaden squirm. She satisfied her lover for the last time. She had her begging and clawing the bed sheets. Dena got off her knees and told Jaden to scoot up in the bed. Jaden moved up and Dena pulled her panties off from under her skirt and got on top of Jaden sixty nine style. She put her pussy in Jaden's face and opened Jaden's pussy and stuck her finger in it. Her head was facing the door. Jaden could not see anything because Dena's ass was on her face. Jaden licked her lovers shaved pussy. Dena moaned when Jaden's tongue penetrated her ass. Dena let Jaden indulge her until she came on her tongue. Jaden was excited that she was able to taste Dena's warm juices and didn't notice Dena's brother sneak into the room. Dena pulled Jaden back down to the end of the bed. Her ass was hanging off the end of the mattress. Dena pointed for her brother to come over to the bed.

Dena took her arms and lifted Jaden's legs and put them under her arms. She licked her thighs and Jaden relaxed. Leon got down on his knees and started licking on Jaden's pussy. Jaden thought she was imagining that Dena's tongue got thicker. She sucked Dena's spur tongue harder and stuck her tongue deep in her pussy. Dena still held Jaden's legs under her arms. She pumped her pussy up and down on Jaden's lips. Her nose was wet from her cum. Dena watched her brother eating Jaden like a pro. She got hot which made her pump harder on Jaden's face. When Leon got up Dena continue licking. Jaden had notice the difference but she was to into Dena's pussy to care. Leon pulled his dick out and dropped his pants. Dena watched with envy. She had seen her brother naked and wished he would fuck her with his large tool. She braced Jaden's legs under her arms and Leon rammed his dick inside her. Jaden screamed she thought the Dena was using a dildo. Then she felt both Dena's hands holding her legs. She tried to push her off her and finally was able to push Dena off to the side. She screamed hard when she saw Leon plunging his dick in her. Dena's other three cousins came in as Jaden started kicking and screaming. The four guys held her arms and legs.

They tied her arms to the post while two guys held her legs up in the air. Dena put a sock in Jaden's mouth then put some duck tape on it. She kissed her on her cheek and said she was sorry. Leon told the other guys to hold her legs higher so he could finish bagging that tight pussy. Tom and George held her legs and Leon indulged in his fantasy of having a black woman. His three minute fantasy came to an end faster then he would have liked to. The thought of fucking a black girl and Jaden's tight virgin pussy made him cum to fast. When Leon got off of her James unzipped his pants. He walked over to the crying, bleeding screaming Jaden and stuck his manhood in her. Jaden yelled and Dena felt sorry for her lover.

"Leon I told you could have her not everybody else." She was trying to get to Jaden but her brother held her back. Jaden yelled and kicked when James forced himself inside her again. He didn't last a minute. "You can't do this Leon she's a virgin she might get pregnant." Dena tried to fight Leon off until he pushed her in the other room. Jaden heard them yelling and screaming at each other trying to take her mind off what was happening to her. The other two guys had their fun with her then they left the room. Leon came back in with Dena on his heels. He wanted some more. Dena begged him no and tried to block him from getting to Jaden he push her away and she hit him. He slapped his sister and pulled his gun out.

"I will put a bullet in her head like I did your other friend."

"Alright don't kill her she's a good person please don't"

"If you don't get out of here I will put a bullet in her now."

Jaden's body had enough she passed out while they were talking. Dena left the room and let her brother have his way with Jaden. She hoped he would keep his word. Leon stayed in the room an hour and violated Jaden in every way possible. She would wake up with him on top of her then she passed back out. When she walk up again she was on her stomach. He took one of her hands loose and did what he wanted until she passed out again. When Leon came out the room he told the guys to get ready so they can leave. He told his sister thanks and threw here a wad of money. Dena didn't catch the money and it hit the floor. When they left Dena went in the room. Tears formed in her eyes when she saw her lover unconscious on the bed blood coming from every hole in her body. Her brother had talked her into setting Jaden up. Last time she did that he killed the girl. Dena was thinking fast. She tried to wake Jaden but was not successful. She put a wet towel on her head and put Jaden's clothes back on. Jaden finally woke up. She was drowsy. Dena slapped her softly. Jaden was hurting all over but she tried to focus on Dena.

"Dena why" is all she could say with tears in her eyes. Dena got her on her feet.

"Jaden we have to get out of here. They're going to kill you when they come back. Can you walk come on Jaden please? I'm so sorry. You got to get out of here." She pulled Jaden and took her to her car. "Can you drive? You have to leave" She put Jaden in the car. Jaden struggled to put her soar body in the car. Dena started the car and hugged her friend. "Jaden I'm so sorry, drive somewhere then call somebody." Dena put her purse on the seat and closed the door. She ran in the house crying. Jaden gathered some strength from inside her. She thought about her mother. She didn't want her to feel any more pain in her life. Jaden put the car in drive and eased off the pedal. The pain from her insides was tearing her up. She moved the car forward slowly. She cried out when the pain was unbearable. She stopped the car waited until the pain went away and drove again. She didn't know how long she was driving she just kept moving. She knew she was on Grand River. The next time the pain hit her she pulled over. She heard her phone vibrate. She put the car in gear painfully and answered the phone.

"Jaden you alright mama is worried about you. Were you at?"

"Jay I been raped" she said in the phone softly. Her twin felt the pain she was feeling and toppled over and screamed. Letha ran in and grabbed the phone. She asked Jaden some questions and told her to go in the mini mall parking lot on Grand River before 7 mile. Jaden said ok, and pulled in the lot. The phone dropped and she passed out. Letha told Momma Cye where she was and we all rushed out the house. We were already on the Westside so we got to her in five minutes. Jaden was slumped over the steering wheel. Momma Cye opened the door. She yelled her name. Aunt Teeka told me to get her out the car. Terrance and I picked her up and put her in the back seat. Momma Cye got in the driver's seat and we rushed her to Botsford hospital that was only a mile away. Momma Cye drove to the emergency entrance and Aunt Teeka went inside and got some doctors. They rushed

Jaden right in. The doctor's closed the doors and told Momma Cye to go to the desk and fill out some paper work. They told us to wait in the waiting room. Jada was hysterical. She was in as much pain as her twin sister. Momma Cye made her go see a doctor and Letha went with her. Aunt Teeka tried to comfort Momma Cye. Her heart was hurting she had has enough pain on her heart. She looked at Aunt Teeka.

"This is it Teeka we can't risk our kids life for something that wasn't their fault." Aunt Teeka agreed. But I thought this was a separate incident. If it had been the Gucci's she would have been dead I thought. We waited for the twins. The doctor's gave Jada some medicine and told her to relax. They ran a rape kit on Jaden and got the DNA from her body. We left the hospital after three hours. Momma Cye, Jada and Jaden went home to relax. Aunt Teeka, Terrance, Letha and I went back to the drug house we were at. Letha wanted to go with us and Aunt Teeka wasn't going to let her go on any mission alone. When we got back to the house it was a lot of crack heads around the house. When we pulled up Terrance and I got out the car and told them to get away from the house and come back in thirty minutes. That's the news they wanted to hear.

The word was that our drugs were good and we gave out big rocks. The dope fiends disbursed and we went in the house. Aunt Teeka and Letha went in the bedroom to talk alone. I think they were trying to figure out what happened to Jaden if that was tied to the Gucci family. Terrance and I prepared for the customers coming back and also if the white guys came back. After twenty minutes the door started ringing. The flow of drug traffic didn't stop for the next two hours. We still were prepared for the uninvited visitors. Aunt Teeka was in one bedroom and Letha in the other. Each one was on the other side of the kitchen. They watched every deal with their guns drawn. I stayed in the kitchen giving out the drugs and Terrance was rough on the door. He was in a bad mood because his girl wasn't feeling good and he couldn't be there with her. He kept his gun out and watched each person that came in with a stern eye. He watched each person leave through the slightly open vertical blinds on the front window. He saw a car pull up when the last person left. He noticed they were white guys inside. He yelled to me special guess coming. I told Letha and Aunt Teeka. Aunt Teeka left out the side door. Three white guys came up to the door the two that were here earlier posing as cops and another man. They knocked on the door. I opened the door while Terrance waited behind the door. The men came in and I partially closed the door. Leaving it open for Aunt Teeka. They walked in and asked.

"Who's in charge here."

"I am what's going on. How can I help you?" I walked pass him going towards the kitchen and put my hand on my gun in my waste. He pushed me to the ground as I walked by. I stumbled over a chair. He went for his gun Letha came out the room and fired one shot. He spun around from the impact of the bullet. I pulled the trigger on my 45 millimeter and two bullets punctured his body. Terrance hit the second in the back of his head with his gun and he fell to the floor. At the same time Aunt Teeka came through the front door and shot the other man in the back of the head just as he was pulling his gun out. All this happened within seconds. Terrance raised his gun to end the life of the man on the floor. Wait Letha yelled.

"Hold up Terrance" she stopped Terrance from killing him. "He looks like a Gucci, search him." She ordered. Terrance and I got the man up and put him in a chair while Aunt Teeka and Letha held their guns on him. The young guy didn't say anything. I reached in his pocket and got his wallet. He had a California driver's license it read James Gucci. I passed the license to Aunt Teeka and Letha. Letha put her gun to his head. Aunt Teeka pulled her hand back just as she was pulling the trigger. The bullet flew pass him and hit the wall. We all had silencers on our weapons so you didn't hear the noise.

"Did you have anything to do with raping my niece?"

The man looked up at them with a puzzled look on his face. He couldn't believed they found out about that so quick. It was only a few hours ago. Aunt Teeka noticed the look on his face and knew he was guilty. Letha wanted to blow his head off but her mother pulled her to the side and talked to her privately. I pushed the man on the floor with the other two men. They were lying in a pool of blood dead. I put my gun to his temple and Terrance pushed his face in the blood. The man screamed like a little bitch. I held his head in the blood with my gun. He saw his life flash before him. He started talking and when I let his head up it was covered with blood. He had to wipe blood of his nose and mouth so he could talk. He was spitting blood that had gone into his mouth as he talked.

"I know what happen but I wasn't involved."

"Who was it?" Letha asked and let off a shot that hit the dead bodies lying next to him. The man shook with fear and peed on himself. He said

"It was my twin cousins Dena and Leon." He told us of how his lesbian cousin Dena set up the girl so her brother could rape her. Then he said "Leon told us we could have her too. I knew he would kill her and us too if we didn't. Afterwards I left and she was still there. Then I came over here."

"How many people raped her?" Letha asked.

"Leon, George, and Tom I couldn't do it." He lied and thought we were stupid enough to buy it. Aunt Teeka looked at me she knew he was lying. But she wanted to hear what he had to say. I asked him where his cousins were now. He told me they were in Farmington. We looked at each other.

"Why my cousin?" Letha shot him in his leg.

"Leon got Dena to do it before in Florida but this time he wanted a black girl and Dena put it in motion." The man held his bleeding leg and pleaded for his life.

"I'm not involved with this please let me go." Aunt Teeka was quiet. She just watched and listened. She remembered reading her husband's appointment book after he was killed. She saw the name Dena on it a few times. The last one on the day he was murdered. Aunt Teeka hit him on the head with the butt of her gun.

"Did Dena set up that lawyer in California too." We all looked at Aunt Teeka we had no idea she connected that part together. The man lowered his head and answered.

"Yes Dena was in on it." He shouldn't have said that. He knew that if they knew about the lawyer then they had to be part of the family they were feuding with or the police. He knew they weren't the police. Aunt Teeka shot him in his knee and in his arm. The man yelled in agony. She pointed the gun at his head. Finish what you were saying or I'll kill you. Give me some good information and I'll let you walk.

"I'm just a cousin I don't know about anybody being killed. Leon made all of us go with him. He said we should revenge our grandparents and fathers life's. I didn't kill anybody. I couldn't pull the trigger when they had the lawyer tied to a bed. I couldn't do it." He started crying. "I couldn't do it"

"Who did it who killed him?" Letha taunted.

"It was Leon, George and Tom my other

cousins." He lied and held his head down begging. Letha looked at the man then at her mother who was crying softly. Letha put the gun to the man's head and told him.

"That was my father" with tears running down her face she shot him three time point blank range. His body fell in the blood of the other two dead men. Aunt Teeka told us that we need to wipe everything down and get out of here. It took us an hour to wipe every inch of the house down. Aunt Teeka found some of that lighter fluid that Letha used earlier. She squirted it on all three bodies. She held her daughters hand and with tears flowing down her cheek she struck a match and dropped threw it on the bodies. The bodies went up in smoke. Letha pulled her mama who stood there dazed watching the flame.

"Mama we got to go." Aunt Teeka wouldn't leave the house until she was sure that each body burned.

Chapter 13

Momma Cye and the twins were sitting in the living room when we arrived back at the house. Terrance was happy to see his girl. He hugged and kissed Jada until Letha told them to get a room. We all laughed and Jaden managed a smile.

"You all right Jaden" Aunt Teeka asked her. I went over and gave my sister a hug and I told her I love her. She smiled. I thought she needed to hear that. We all sat up and watched movies and ate popcorn. No one said anything about the events of the day. We wanted the day to pass so we could plan for tomorrow. Jaden was gaining her strength as the days passed by. For the rest of us it was business as usual. Letha, Jada, Terrance and I checked on our drug business and opened another house on the Westside. It was a couple of months since Jaden was raped. I noticed the way Jada was now dressing like her sister. Jada use to dress up skinny jeans, pumps and a nice expensive blouse. Now she dressed like her sister a college student. She wore baggy jeans, gym shoes or sandals. She wore her hair like Jaden up in a ponytail. Put she still wore her makeup which made her glow and she still kept her gun in her purse. Both twins were very nice looking and could turn any man's head.

I never questioned why Jada did this. I thought she wanted to be like her sister. After we checked on the houses we went shopping at the mall. Terrance and I wanted to check out some Timberlines so we told the girls to meet us in one hour by the Bose Store. We were in Summerset Mall. Terrance and I shopped for about forty five minutes and waited for the girls to come out. We went into the Bose store to look around and listen to music with their surround sound. Terrance was talking to the salesman when the girls came out. I saw them being approached by a white girls. The girl talked to Jada . Letha turned around and looked at me staring at her through the window. She gave me a sign with her hand to hold up be cool. I knew something was going on. When the girl saw Jada in the store she couldn't believe her eyes. She waited until she came out the store to make sure it was her. Dena thought she looked like her friend. But this girl had a natural glow that she never saw before. When Jada came out the store with Letha the girl looked to make sure. She approached them.

"Jaden is that you?" Jada kept walking and talking to Letha. "Jaden don't do this to me I'm sorry." Jada turned around she was hoping it was who she thought it was. She had to be sure she never saw the woman before. "Jaden please don't ignore me I am so sorry."

Letha spun around with a hand in her purse holding her gun. She didn't know what was happening. Jada was in complete control. She patted her cousin on the hand looked in her eyes in her eyes to tell her everything was cool.

"Jaden please don't do this to me after all we been through. You know I love you a lot. I'm sorry"

"Dena I'm not talking to you. I need time to get over what you did to me." Jada took a chance that she was Dena the girl that set her twin sister up to be raped.

"Alright Jaden, please forgive me. My brother made me do it. It was his idea you know I care about you."

Letha was behind her listening to the bull shit she was running. She put her hand back in her purse. Jada had an eye on Letha who stood behind the woman. She shook her head no to Letha. The woman didn't know how close she was to death at that moment.

"I'm madder at you Dena then your brother. You could have warned me. Your brother made me feel better than you ever could. I got to go." Jada said and walked away with Letha. She made Dena feel bad. She picked up her cell phone called me and told me to follow Dena. She said she would call her mother to pick them up. I told Terrance to go get the car and I followed the woman to her car. Letha called me back and said don't do anything to her because Jada had a plan.

The Gucci cousins were in California attending the funeral of James Gucci. After the funeral Leon got all his cousins together. He told them that they need to come with him to revenge their family's deaths. He said it wasn't fair that we suffer so much and the other family they're feuding with don't. One cousin declined. He said every time they go to Detroit somebody comes home dead. He wanted to live his life. Leon couldn't recruit any more family members and left California with Tom and George. When they arrived Leon called his sister Dena. She couldn't wait to tell him about Jaden. She told him she ran into her at a Mall and she wasn't mad. She told him that she talked about how he satisfied her so well. Dena was stroking her brothers' ego. She knew that if she didn't get Jaden to come around then her brother could. Leon had his own idea. He wanted to get with Jaden again. She is all he has been thinking about. He touched his crouch. That was the best pussy he ever had. He wouldn't mind having it on a continuous basis. Dena thought about Jaden and her making love again like they use to. He told his sister to see if she could hook up with her. Tell her that he was sorry they met that way but he would like to take her shopping and dinner to make up. Dena couldn't wait to call Jaden. She could use Leon as an excuse. How she thought that Jaden wanted to talk to the man that rape her was beyond me. She picked up her cell phone and called Jaden. The phone rang over and over she dialed it six more times only to hear it keep ringing. Dena never noticed the car following her. Terrance and I stayed back a distance. We watched her drive to a nice Bloomfield home. Terrance wrote down the address. We watched the house for a couple of hours and left. There were a few cars in the drive way but we didn't notice any other movement.

Jada had called her mother to come pick her up at the mail. Aunt Teeka and Jaden rode with her. When Jada and Letha got into the car they were asked a lot of questions. Jada told them about her encounter with Dena. Aunt Teeka turned around in disbelieve. She knew that Dena had set up her husband to be killed.

"What you guys saw her and let her go." She asked her daughter and niece.

"She thought I was Jaden. She had the nerve to say she was sorry and wanted to know if we could hook up." Jada looked at her sister who started crying. "Jaden I want to handle this. When Dena calls just keep leading her on. I told her that you wanted to see her brother again. So we can get both of them at the same time. I'm sorry sis but she approached me." Jada held her sister and they both cried softly. Momma Cye said that she thought Jada's plan might work since the girl didn't know she had a twin sister. Both Momma Cye and Aunt Teeka said they wanted to be there when they met up with them.

When we arrived back at the house I was surprise to see Marketta. She was talking to Jaden and Aunt Teeka. Momma Cye was in the kitchen cooking. I know I haven't been home in a few days dealing with the families crises. But I never thought my woman would come look for me. Terrance was happy to see his sister and teased me about her.

"Man what you do to my sister got her chasing you down. What's up Ketta you alright?"

"Hi Tee you keeping my man away from me." They both laughed and she gave me the biggest hug. I missed her I didn't realized that I haven't seen her in a week. The girls went upstairs like they usually do to talk girl talk. Terrance and I went downstairs to count the money we been staking. We were sitting down in the cellar smoking some blunts and talking. We had about three hundred and eighty thousand dollars. We still had enough product from the large buy to bring in another half million. Terrance passed me the joint looked at me and asked me truthfully.

"RJ, when do we ever stop? You know I'm down with whatever we have to do. But when are we going to be able to enjoy some of this."

"Terrance I hope this ends soon. I want to be able to spend my life with Marketta." Almost on cue the door to the cellar open and it was Marketta. She never came down there before but I was glad she did. Now I can get Terrance to roll out and I might be able to knock that body for some sex.

"Hi baby, you want to hit this joint" I asked.

"No baby I don't want any. I just missed you RJ."

"Come on Ketta this shit is good relax a little." Terrance pushed the joint in her face.

"Do you want your nephew or niece to smoke weed." I looked at Terrance for a response. I was so high I didn't get what was going on. Terrance looked at me he started laughing. Marketta held my hand and waited for my reaction.

"Boy you better man up." He said and hit me on the back. I either was too high or I never imaged anything like that could happen to me. Marketta said to me.

"RJ I'm pregnant with your child. I'm sorry I didn't mean for it to happen." She started crying.

"What I'm going to be a father, no shit." I said. Marketta held me and looked in my eyes.

"If we have this baby please don't ever leave me. I don't want to raise a kid by myself. Me and my brother lived with one parent all our life's. I don't want my kid to go through that."

"I love you Marketta I will never leave you alone."

"I'm going upstairs you're blowing my high with all this love shit. Going to find my girl."

Terrance had his hand on his grouch and got up to leave.

"Terrance you just plain nasty." Marketta said.

"I'm the one nasty, you babying up my boy." We all laughed. Terrance disappeared up the stairs. I kissed Marketta hard and felt her warm breath reaching the love line I have in my heart for her. I really missed her. I rubbed her chest and pulled one titty out and kissed it softly. She smiled at me and took her blouse and bra off. Her chest bounced up and down as she moved slowly teasing me with her movements. She turned around and lowered her pants down to her ankles. She looked at me through her open legs seductively while slowly removing her panties. She stepped out of her pants and panties and put her finger in her mouth arousing me as I watched her intently. She walked over to me naked as a jay bird and bent over in front of me grabbing her ankles. Her ass was almost in my face. I good see the juices of her excitement flowing out her small wonderland of pinkness. I was totally aroused. I pulled her butt cheeks to my face and stuck my long tongue as far as I could inside her pussy. She moaned with excitement. I licked the side of her pink playhouse and spread her open with my fingers. She parted her legs and pushed her ass on my tongue. I stuck my tongue inside her again and moved it from side to side. She fucked my tongue to my movements until she let out a scream of ecstasy as she climaxed on my face. I continued to lick the juices and she pushed her ass deeper in my face until she couldn't take any more. She screamed with excitement and tried to pull away. I had her by her hips and held her in my grip until she came on my face again. She said my name softly and also said she loved me. I stood up and unzipped my pants keeping my thumb inside her pussy. I pulled my dick out and stuck it deep inside her. I felt the walls of her vagina collapse on my hard dick. I put my hips in every stroke and hit her on the ass with my hand. "Whose pussy is this?" I asked while plunging with force. "Whose pussy is this?" I asked again.

"Is your daddy, it's your pussy?" she moaned. Her white ass turned red as I smacked it harder. She grimaced in pain and enjoyed the pleasure at the same time. She was getting turned by my words. "Gimmy that pussy, show me it's mine."

"Here it's yours RJ, nobodies put yours."
I pulled out of her and laid her back on the recliner seat I was sitting on. I pushed the chair all the way back. She laid back and opened up her legs. I put my arms under her legs and held her

legs wider apart. I rammed myself inside her until I couldn't go any further. I was hitting the bottom. She grabbed her toes opened her legs as far as they would go. Although she was in pain she looked at me with those big hazel brown eyes and said.

"RJ I'm totally yours you can have me any way you want me anytime you want me. I love you." The words from her mouth took me to a higher level and I couldn't hold it any longer.

"I love you too, Marketta and I will always be with you and our child forever." I came inside her so long that I got an instant headache. That was one of the best nuts I've had. I welcomed the headache. We laid there in our afterglow looking into each other's eyes. I kissed her passionately.

"Are you really going to have my baby?"

"If you really want me to I'll have your child."

"That would make me so happy. I could get out of the game and we can leave comfortable."

"That's your decision. I'll love you anyway." The door to the basement opened and we scrambled to put our close on just as Terrance was coming down the stairs. He looked at us.

"It smells like pussy down here. You making babies down here Ketta? Now that's just nasty." We all started laughing. We went upstairs and I went and took a shower. The bathroom door opened it was Marketta she jumped in the shower with me and we went for round two. When we came downstairs everybody was looking at us funny. I guess it showed on our face happiness and satisfaction. Letha, Jada, Jaden, Aunt Teeka and Momma Cye just looked at us smiling.

"Are you going to give me a grandchild?" Momma Cye asked as everybody wanted for the answer. I knew Terrance had told Jada, who told Letha and her mother who told Aunt Teeka. It was out.

"Yes Momma Cye Marketta is pregnant and we decided we are going to keep the child."

"You have made me so happy." Momma Cye rushed over and hugged Marketta and me. I blushed at the thought of being a daddy. I knew my life had to change. The girls took Marketta and went upstairs. Aunt Teeka and Momma Cye went shopping. The baby wasn't even two months in her stomach and they wanted to go shopping. I will never understand women. Terrance and I went to check on our money. Usually when Marketta comes over we let the girls have their time together. So we went to check on our houses. I was really excited to get back on the street because I knew I had to get my hustle on so I can step out the game with a truck full of money. When we arrived at the first house we picked up about eight thousand dollars. We put the money in a leather bag. Then we headed for our next house. When we got to the house on the Westside the guys act like they didn't want to let us in. When we asked for the money they said they were short. Terrance pulled his gun out but the guy holding the shot gun had his gun pointed towards Terrance. I didn't draw my gun.

"Hold on everybody be cool. We just come to collect."

"Tell him to drop his gun" The guy with the rifle said."

"You pulling a gun on me and you work for me."

"I work for Steve he hired me" the man yelled.

"Steve what's going on? You got our money?" I asked.

"RJ we just a little short come back later I'll have it."

"What kind of shit you talking. You aint got our shit." Terrance looked at me. He was ready to blast our way out of there. My thinking had changed since I knew I was going to be a father. I want my kid to know me unlike my dad who didn't get to know me.

"Hold up T, We'll give them one hour to have our money. We will be back in one hour. Have our shit."

Terrance looked at the man and I knew he was going to kill him if not now later. You can't let someone pull a gun out on you and don't use it. It shows weakness. The guy with the shot gun opened the door and still had the gun on Terrance. Terrance looked him in his eyes. The man was so loyal to Steve he didn't know what was going on. Terrance put his gun up and we walked out the door. I waited until I got to the car and called Letha. We drove up the block like we were leaving but we could still see the house from where we parked at. Letha, Jada. Aunt Teeka and Momma Cye arrived in ten minutes. I didn't want her to bring them but I'm sure they insisted on coming. They couldn't stop their mothers's especially these two. As soon as they pulled up I saw two cars of guys drive up to the house. They got out I noticed one of my competitors with them.

"That's Andre what the fuck is he doing here?"

"I knew I recognized the guy with the shotgun. RJ he works for Andre. He is one of his henchmen." Terrance chimed in. The door to

Terrance's chevy sedan opened and the ladies got in. We all squeezed in. I told them what we just witnessed. Aunt Teeka said let's wait and see what happens before we go in. Momma Cye said we need a plan. It was six guys in the house waiting on us to come back. We waited for a while. The door opened about fifteen minutes before we were to return. Three guys came out the house and went to move the cars. One guy took one of the cars around the back of the house. Two guys parked the car on the other side of the street from the house. We talked to devise a plan. This was a new house that Terrance and I set up. So they never saw the girls. Benefits for having women down in your crew is rewarding. Aunt Teeka reached in her bag and pulled out two 45 millimeter guns with silencers. She gave one to me and the other to Terrance. Letha started to get out.

"Where are you going? Wait a minute." Aunt Teeka pulled her hand. She closed the door back. "We don't know if these guys have seen you before. Guys check you out and you don't know they are looking. If that's your competitor he has seen all of you. That's why he thinks he could take you and take over your business."

Aunt Teeka was making sense. Her and Momma

Cye's experience has kept us alive so many times. We had to listen to them and learn. We were parked a half of block behind the car on the other side of the street from the house. Aunt Teeka and Momma Cye got out the car. Momma Cye walked ahead of Aunt Teeka. She reached the car and knocked on the window. The guy on the passenger side looked at Momma Cye. She had a low cut blouse on under her coat and when she bent down her cleavage showed.

"Could you tell me where I can cop some coke?" The window was halfway down and both men looked at her chest instead of watching her hand movement.

"No we don't know so get away from the car." The driver said. Momma Cye backed up and with a quick motion pulled her 9 millimeter and fire three shots hitting the man in the head. The driver had his gun on his lap and picked it up just as he felt the hot lead penetrate the back of his head. Aunt Teeka pulled the trigger twice and the man slumped to the side. Both men laid slumping down on each other. Aunt Teeka motioned for us and Terrance and I came to the car and were told to push the bodies in the back seat. We put on our gloves and tried not to get any blood on us. The bullets put holes in the dash board and the others stayed in their bodies. So there wasn't a lot of blood. Terrance and I pushed the bodies in the back seat. Then we all went back to Terrance's car and drove around the block and came to the back of the house through the ally. Terrance stopped the car when he saw a man at the back of the house with his gun out. He was peeking around watching the front of the house and smoking a cigarette. Jada and Letha got out the car and walked up the alley towards the house. The guy turned around and saw the two girls laughing and talking before he could say anything. Jada asked him if she could buy a cigarette. He looked at Jada then looked at Letha. He knew he had seen her before but couldn't think where.

"Come on man, I'll give you five dollars my husband made me stop smoking and now I need a smoke." Jada reached in her pocket and gave the man five dollars. The man reached in his pocket to get a cigarette just as Letha brought her gun with the silencer on it and shot him in the chest. Jada pulled her gun and shot him in the face. The man fell against the house his body slid down the side of the house and hit the ground. Jada searched his pockets and found the keys to his car. I got out the car got took the keys. I drove the car around to the front of the house. I backed in so the guys in the house could see the car but not who was in it. Terrance parked the car in the alley and everybody walked to the house. Jada and Momma Cye stayed by the side door. I knew that the bathroom was by the side door and I told Letha. Letha, Aunt Teeka and Terrance knocked on the door. There were three men inside Andre, the man with the shot gun and Steve. The door opened and they walked in. The man with the shot gun stood behind the door after he closed it. Andre looked at them and asked where I was.

"I have to go to the bathroom bad. Can I use it?" Aunt Teeka asked holding her legs together like she was going to pee on herself. Andre looked at her and figured that her old ass wasn't going to do anything. He motioned for her to go ahead. Aunt Teeka ran to the bathroom still holding her legs together. She slipped the lock off the side door and let Momma Cye and Jada in.

"So where is RJ? I got a business venture for him."

Before Terrance could answer there was a knock on the door. Steve pulled his gun out and put it on the table he and Andre were sitting at. The guy with the shot gun looked out the window. He saw both cars so he knew his men would be right behind RJ when he came in. He opened the door and RJ came in. Andre's eyes were on RJ and he didn't notice Steve slumped down in his chair.

"Don't anybody move." Aunt Teeka said. Andre turned and saw three guns pointed at his head. Jada's gun was against his temple. He looked at Steve face fell on the table with a bullet hole in the back of his head. The guy with the shot gun cocked his gun. Terrance turned and shot him in his knee he buckled and fell to the floor. He shouted in pain. Andre didn't speak he knew any moment that his other guys would be coming in soon.

"So what kind of business venture you had for RJ?" Terrance asked Andre. He looked around and thought he should choose his words wisely. I walked over to where he was sitting. Kicked Steve's chair when he fell to the ground. I picked up his chair and sat down next to Andre then asked.

"What kind of business you got for me Andre. I hope it's not the some kind your three dead partners have."

Andre swallowed hard. Old school drug dealers had told him not to come at us but he thought we didn't have a crew to handle him. He didn't know that everybody in our crew was trained to kill all of us natural killers. He looked at his soldier bleeding and holding his leg. Terrance looked at the guy and smiled.

"You know you shouldn't pull a gun on someone and don't use it."

Terrance shot the man again and watched him yell. He enjoy his pain. Then Terrance shot him twice in the chest to end his suffering. Andre looked stunned.

"If you waiting on your crew outside. They're dead. Now, what you want to talk to me about. I know you don't have enough nerve to step to me on your own."

"Let me blow his head off." Letha said and cocked her gun then pushed the cold steel barrel to his head.

"Hold up man, Ok I got in dept with this white boy and he told me I could squash the dept if I took over this house." Andre said. Letha hit him in his face with her gun butt. Blood shot out the big gash it left in his forehead.

"What's the white boys name?" She asked raring back to hit him again. He put his hand up in defense.

"His name is Leon. Leon Gucci" he held his head down. Everybody looked at each other for a split second letting his words sink in. Then we heard two thumps from a silencer. Momma Cye was standing behind Andre with her gun smoking. Jada shot him in the chest just in case the lord didn't think he was ready. No more words were said. I looked around for any drugs or money. The women cleaned the house down. Even though we all had on gloves Terrance and I had been in the house before and might have left our finger prints.

Chapter 14

When we got back to the house Jaden was sitting on the couch. She looked sad. Jada asked her what was wrong and she said that Dena had called her. She said that they had been talking about a week and Dena was really is trying to get them to hook up again. It only made he think about when she was raped. Her sister consoled her.

"Did she want to meet up with you?"

"I don't think I could face her Jada and pretend like nothing happened. I can't do it."

"You don't have to. I will go in your place. You just keep stringing her along and when the time is right we will meet her and her brother."

"And I'll make sure that he doesn't rape

again." Momma Cye said as she hugged her twin daughters. Terrance, Letha and I went down stairs to count the money we got out of the house and on the dead bodies. We opened the hideaway door and counted the money. We counted the eight thousand five hundred dollars threw it in a large garbage can we had full of bundles of money. We pulled the drugs out and counted the kilo's. We still had 22 kilos left. We had to get rid of the drugs. I told Letha my intentions of leaving the game. She said she was tired too. She wanted to go somewhere and live with her mother and Aunts. So we all agreed at that time that this was the last drugs that we buy and sale. We gave out selves six to eight months to sell out and another month to get all our money off the street. Jada came down stairs after we had put up everything. She had Jaden and Marketta with her. We broke out the table and started playing cards.

A few months pasted without incident. The four of us was on the street selling and picking up cash. Aunt Teeka and Momma Cye would always follow us. And have our backs. It was like a nine to five. We left early in the morning and returned home to eat dinner in the evening. Jaden usually had dinner made for us. She was beginning to get back to her old self. She started to ride with us because she was bored at home. The money in the basement was mounting up. We had at least three large garbage cans full of money. Momma Cye went in the basement and organized and counted all the money. She divided it up seven times. Each one of us had I million two hundred eighty thousand each. Momma Cye took each one of us separately and had us open a safe deposit box all in different banks. She then called her contact for an off shore account and made us put in half a million each in an account with our name on it with one person in the family the beneficiary. We were millionaires put Aunt Teeka taught us not to flaunt. We drove old cars never wore flashy jewelry and we stayed together. We didn't allow anyone else to come into our circle. Marketta and Jaden became best of friends. I think it was there experience in college that made them bond. Jada found out she was pregnant. So the girls always went shopping with Terrance and I trailing along. We dropped Marketta off at her house. Jada had a craving for some peanuts. She was only two months pregnant but she still had cravings all the time. We stopped at a gas station. Jada and her sister got out. Letha didn't want anything so she stayed in the car. After a couple of minutes Jaden came out running to the car. Letha and I jumped out car and held her. In tears she yelled

"He's in there he's in there" she screamed as she shook with fear.

"Who's in there?" Letha asked while she reached in the car for her purse.

"One of the guys that raped me. She screamed. Terrance was already heading for the door. I ran behind him. Letha stayed outside to console Jaden. When I walked in the guy was talking to Jada in a corner. Terrance picked a magazine and made eye contact with Jada. She smiled letting Terrance know she was alright. The guy she was talking to thought she was smiling at him. How could he rape my sister and possibly think she was alright with it I thought. He had the wrong opinion of black girls. Leon had told him what Dena had said. So he thought she might want to get with him. Are white people really that stupid? Jada was talking to him like he was a friend. My cell rang. It was Letha she told me to come out so we could follow him. I motioned for Terrance and we both went outside. Letha and Jaden walked to the corner. Terrance and I got in the car and pulled off the gas station lot.

"Dena really misses you. When you coming

by?" The gentleman asked Jada.

" I've been talking to Dena, Can I ask you something." Jada didn't give him time to answer. "Did you enjoy raping me." Jada had a smirk on her face but she wanted to know if he enjoyed raping her sister.

"I didn't want to do it. No I didn't enjoy it. I sometimes wonder how it would have been if we meet on different circumstances. I'm so sorry it happen. But Leon would have killed me if I didn't. I told Dena to tell you I was sorry." Jada had tears in her eyes when Letha came in the gas station. She had just put her hand in her purse touching her gun. Instead she picked up her cell phone that was ringing. It was Letha she told Jada to let him leave and that we were going to follow him. Jada listened but still she wanted to kill him. Letha hung up the phone when she reached Jada's side. She grabbed her by the arm.

"Come on Jaden what's taking you so long."

"I got to go. Tell Dena to call me." Jada said acting like she was her twin Jaden.

"Here's my number, you can call me." The man gave her a card with his number on it and left the gas station. Jada got some peanuts and paid for them. When the girls left the gas station the men was already gone. Terrance and I followed him. Aunt Teeka and Momma Cye picked all three of the girls up. Letha called me and I communicated where we were. We were driving by the airport. it looked like he was heading to the airport. But he made a turn and went to Romulus a suburb in Michigan. He pulled up to a house that was near a secluded area. There wasn't another house for blocks. The guy got out. Jada had told me the card read Tom Gucci. Terrance and I sat on the house watching every movement. We weren't sure how many people were in the house because Tom pulled in the garage before we could get close enough to look in. Aunt Teeka pulled up next to me with the girls and Momma Cye in the car with her. We moved to a lot down the road where we could still see the house and anybody coming or going. After an hour Jada said she had an idea. She wanted to call him and see if he would invite her over. We all didn't like the idea because if someone else was there it could be another set up. Jada said the guy was stupid and she knew she could play on his emotions. She said he wasn't thinking with the right head. We asked Jaden what she thought and let her make the decision. Jaden told her sister to call.

"Hi is this Tom? This Jaden we met earlier."

" Hi Jaden I was hoping you would call me."

" I was thinking about what you said. About different circumstances, and I'd like to start over." Tom thought about it for a minute. Then his ego got in the way. He forgot how he violated her. He was thinking that she liked him and he could brag in front of his cousins and have this dime piece on his arm. So what if they fucked her before. He would be the one fucking her now. He smiled at his thoughts.

"I knew you liked me. What you doing?"

" I'm on Wayne road waiting on my cousin she had some errands to run. So I called you."

"I live a couple blocks from there." Jada was quite. She let him think for a few minutes.

"I know this sounds crazy put I want to see you and talk to you. You said different circumstances. I want you to give me a chance." Jada smiled she knew she had him.

"I'm on Wayne Rd. are you going to come get me."Momma Cye was shaking her head no.

"Where at on Wayne road" Jada was quite. She looked at her mother and held up a finger.

"Hold on my cousin going to drop me off. But she said she'll be back in an hour to pick me up. I don't know about this, I don't want what happened before to happen again. I don't think

I'm going to come by. We can talk on the phone.

"Jaden nobody is here but me. This is my house and I'm alone. Just come talk to me for an hour. I promise to be nothing but a gentleman." Jada was quite again. Tom's mind was moving he really wanted to get to know Jaden. "Ok just come by for a half an hour. I just want to talk to you get to know you and your life." This guy was almost begging Jada had him where she wanted him.

"I will have my cousin drop me off and in thirty minutes she will be knocking on the door. If anything happens to me she is going to call the police and my family."

"I assure you nothing is going to happen." Jada asked him for the address and hung up. Momma Cye warned Jada to keep her eyes open. Don't drink anything and try to get him to open up to you about his family. Find out if he has a gun on him. We will be at that door in twenty minutes. If no one opens the door when we knock then we start shooting. Please be careful baby. Momma Cye, Aunt Teeka and Jaden got in the car with Terrance and me. Letha drove to drop Jada off. I asked Jada if she was packing. She told me always. We watched the car Letha was driving drop Jada off. On the inside Jada was welcomed by Tom Gucci. He was very nice trying to make her comfortable. Jada asked him questions about him and his family. After ten minutes Tom asked Jada if she could come to a cook out with all his family on the fourth of July. That was a jack pot as far as Jada was concern. She told him maybe and asked him where. He told her in Bloomfield and gave her the address just in case she could make it. Twenty minutes passed. It was time for us to role. I was nervous for Jada and I think everybody was ready to get in there. Jaden got in the car with Letha. Aunt Teeka told us to go park on the side of the house where the garage was. She thought if he was by himself his attention would be on Jada and wouldn't notice the car pulling on the lot. That was the longest twenty minutes for all of us especially Jaden who was worried about her sister. Letha drove on the lot. Jaden and her got out. Letha waited on the side of the door with her gun out as Jaden knocked. Inside Tom Gucci and Jada were sitting at the dining room table. When Jada heard the knock she asked could she use the restroom. She went to the restroom and Tom went to answer the door. He opened the door and was confused. He looked back to see Jada standing there. Then he looked back at Jaden at the door. He knew something wasn't right but in his mind he thought he was in heaven. Two fine black girls. Then he noticed the gun in Jada's hand. We all wanted to rush in but Momma Cye told us to wait. She said that she wanted Jaden to do what she had to do so that she could stop feeling so bad. As Tom closed the door he again looked at the girls. Then it finally hit him he was set up.

"What's the gun for I didn't touch you Jaden."

"I'm Jaden" Tom turned to Jaden he froze. "I'm the one you raped." He backed up to the closed door and tried to reach to his back for his gun. Jaden pulled an ice pick from her jacket pocket and stuck him in his neck. She stuck him again and again. Blood gushing out on her hand and face but she kept stabbing him. He was sliding down the door and Jaden keep pulling the ice pick out and re asserting it in his body. Jada came to her sister's side and shot Tom in his head and grabbed her sister and they hugged for a long time. Terrance and I pushed the front door hard to get in. Momma Cye and Aunt Teeka rushed in to see the dead man on the floor. Terrance hugged Jada and I hugged my sister Jaden.

"It's over Jaden" I whispered in her ear. She held my tight and said.

"It's just beginning big bro." The look in her

eyes was one of relief and determination. She was more determined to get the other guys who raped her. Aunt Teeka asked Jada did she touch anything. When she said no we left but not before I took the ice pick out of the dead body of Tom Gucci.

Chapter 15

When we got back to the house Jaden was still upset. I don't think it was because she had killed a man. I think it was emotionally just looking at the guy that violated her. Jada made sure her sister was alright before she left with Terrance. They went back to their apartment. I went over Marketta's to spend some time with her. Momma Cye and Aunt Teeka cooked some dinner and talked. It always amazed me that a day of killing someone was as normal to our family as picking up the newspaper. We sometimes didn't even mention what had happen while we were in the streets. The weird thing was that our parents didn't either. Unless we did something wrong where we would have put one of our lives in jeopardy. Jaden and Letha went up stairs. Letha was trying to be there for Jaden. Since she was also molested she understood where she was coming from. Letha and Jaden were sitting on the edge of the bed. Jaden put her head in Letha's lap. She asked Letha what happened when she got raped. Letha had never told her story to anybody. She had kept it in trying to pretend it never happen. But since Jaden had went through it she told Jaden what happen that night she was kidnapped and left for dead. She never told anyone that she was raped by three men. Letha let it all out and told Jaden every detail. When she got through she was crying but talking about it was a burden off her shoulders.

"I'm going to take a shower." Letha said as she started taking her clothes off. She stripped down her patties and walked in the bathroom. She was still a little emotional and cried softly as she got in the shower. Jaden felt her pain. She locked the bedroom door and took all her clothes off and went in to the bathroom. Letha had her head under the shower letting the hot water flow down her body. Jaden got in and held her from behind. Both girls cried uncontrollable. As if they were letting out the demons of each of the men that took what they wanted from them. Jaden begin to kiss Letha's back. Letha didn't move she let her warm tongue and the hot water sooth her inside. Jaden tenderly kiss Letha all over her back and her ass cheeks. Letha didn't resist. It had been a long time since any one touched her body. With each kiss Letha thought about the only guy she ever had Rick. He was killed in front of her before she was raped. Letha sobbed as she vision the man pulling the trigger and Ricks head after the impact of the bullet left one single hole in his forehead. Jaden's tongue soothed her thoughts and she let herself go. She didn't think anything else the hot water and Jaden's mellow touch was doing wonders to her body. Jaden licked her legs and her thighs then she got in front of Letha. The water running down her face coming off Letha's body had Jaden hot with passion. She got on her knees and let her tongue run up Letha's legs. She licked her thighs and moved straight up to the soft lips of her pussy. Letha moaned at the feeling she never had. Jaden was a master and Letha opened her legs giving Jaden full access to her wanting body. Letha never gave it a thought about what she was doing. She only yearned for the sexual desire Jaden was giving her. Jaden used her tongue with perfection and had Letha backing away. She backed to the shower wall and slide down and sat on the tub. Jaden put one of Letha's legs on the top of the tub and she laid down inside the tub. She took her fingers and spread Letha's pussy lips open getting excited looking at her pink insides. She sucked her clit tenderly. Letha let out a soft yell. Jaden ran he tongue up and down her pussy. Then stuck her tongue into her as far as it would go Letha shivered with pleasure. Jaden made Letha's climax. She was a virgin to a warm tongue and Jaden was breaking her in and out. Letha was at Jaden's mercy and she couldn't break lose. Jaden sucked and licked on Letha for over an hour. Then they got out the tub. Jaden put lotion all on Letha's body and again let her tongue fore fill all of Letha's desires. Letha's mind and body was so relaxed that they fell asleep in each other's arms.

In Romulus Leon Gucci had found the body of his cousin. He was pissed and took it out on any one that was around him. His other cousin was almost shot when Leon started shooting recklessly. He wanted revenge for this and he could only think of one person responsible for this. The girl they had raped. He knew he should have killed her. His sister stopped him. He picked up the phone and called his sister Dena. "Dena, Tom is dead. Someone shot him and stabbed him. He has holes in throat."

"What who would do that to him. He didn't even know anybody here. Who did it?"

"I bet that bitch Jaden had something to do with it. I knew I should have killed her."

"Why you think Jaden would do that?"

"I just got a feeling. Have you talked to her?"

" Yes I talked to her yesterday. She has forgiven us. She wants to go on with her life."

"I want you to set up a meeting. I'll ask her myself if she had something to do with this."

"No Leon I won't. You are going to hurt her."

" Whose side you on. She killed your cousin you are defending her? You my family."

Dena thought for a minute and knew her brother was right. But she wasn't sure that Jaden did or could do anything like that. She didn't know much about Jaden's family because she didn't talk much about them.

"Ok, I told her I wanted her to come over the fourth of July and she agreed."

"What you going to bring her around family?"

" Yes, you can talk to her then. I know you

won't kill her in front of family like that. If she don't know anything about it I could enjoy her company. You take that or don't see her at all."

"I can't believe you got caught up on that dike. Bring her then if she knows something I am going to take her out back and put two in her skull. After I fuck the shit out of her first."

"Fuck you Leon, She is not like that she couldn't kill anybody in cold blood." Dena hung the phone up and called Jaden. The cell phone ringing woke Letha up. She laid there and let it ring. She thought about Jaden and how good she made her fill. Letha didn't think she liked woman but she never had been interested in men. The phone brought her out her thoughts. She looked in Jaden's purse and found her cell phone. She saw on the caller ID it was Dena. She woke Jaden up and gave her the phone. Jaden put the phone on speaker. She told Dena she just woke up. Dena begged her to reconsider coming over on the fourth of July. Jaden had already said no.

"Please say you would come Jaden."

"I don't know Dena I told you I might come."

"My whole family will be there. I want you to meet them. My brother will be there too. He said he wanted to apologize to you in person."

Jaden thought to herself the nerve some white

folks have. Saying I'm sorry won't make me feel any better. I want him to feel what I felt.

"Alright Dena I'll come only if I can bring my cousin. Is she welcome to come?" Jaden asked.

"Sure she is. The address is 75 Lakewood Dr."

"I'll see you Saturday about 4:00 o'clock. I have to spend time with my family also."

"Every part of me will be waiting on you." Dena hung up the phone and smiled at the thought of holding and touching Jaden again. She thought she would never get that opportunity again. Jaden hung up the phone and looked at Letha. Her mind was on her plan. If they planned it right they could get all the Gucci family and this whole scenario that has lasted twenty five years would end one way or another. Jaden hit hand.

"What you thinking about. You got a plan?"

"Yes I do call Jada and tell her. I'll call RJ and we will have a meeting tomorrow." Letha got up and went downstairs where Momma Cye and her mother Aunt Teeka were in the kitchen eating.

"Mama why didn't you call me to eat?"

"You kids are grown I'm not chasing you down to make you eat. You could smell the food cooking." Letha just smiled her mother was right. Letha got a plate and fixed her something to eat. Jaden came down stairs hugged her mother and sat down and ate. An hour later Jada and Terrance came over and they called me to join them. Since everybody was there but me they said we should have the meeting tonight. When I got there everyone was sitting in the living room. They all looked so serious. We started the meeting off by each person telling what they knew about the Gucci's and if they felt the time had come to end the feuding. Aunt Teeka started by telling us how this all got started she broke down when she talked about Letha's father Carl and her mother Aunt Lolo. She also told us about the deaths of her crew making sure she stayed alive by sacrificing theirs own lives. Momma Cyr talked about her parent's death and how her life spiraled downhill. Each person gave their virgin of how they felt. When we were all done we all devised a plan. We also took time and prayed. We prayed that everybody would come home alive. It was four in the morning before we stopped our meeting. We had breakfast and spent the next day getting our arsenal together. Although we didn't have much time before the fourth of July Aunt Teeka hoped she could find a way into the house without us coming through the front door. It was Monday and the fourth was Saturday. On Wednesday Aunt Teeka's phone rang and she got the information she was waiting on. Momma Cye told all of us to spend time to ourselves for a couple of days. Marketta and I went baby shopping with Jada and Terrance. Letha and Jaden stayed together getting to know each other. We all had an idea that they were liking each other. They were always smiling and laughing and enjoying each other's company. Momma Cye and Aunt Teeka stayed at home going through paper work and making sure all monies were divided. All of our drugs were out so Terrance and I dropped the girls off and went to pick up any money we had on the street. We went to the first three houses and collected our money. Two of them were out of drugs and we told them we were waiting on a shipment. As we drove up to the last house we noticed three white guys coming out. Terrance kept driving. We drove around the block and parked down the street were we could see them. The white guys came out and then went back in. When they came out again they had our black bag that I'm sure was full of money. They also had their guns out. They got in their cars and drove off. Terrance and I decided we were going to wait and see what happens. At this point we didn't want to jeopardize our plans for the fourth of July. We didn't want to let our family down. We were the only guys left and we had to take care of them. After the guys were gone for fifteen minutes we went inside. I had my gun out and so did Terrance. When we got inside we couldn't believe what we saw. The two guys watching the house were in the bedroom. But their heads were in the kitchen. One torso was on the bed with blood splattered on the floors and walls. The other torso was slumped in a chair blood running down the front of his body to the floor. Terrance and I searched the house then left in a hurry. There was nothing we could do. At this point our focus was on getting out the game and staying alive to raise our unborn kids.

Although we all were told to spend time by ourselves Thursday we were all back home. Aunt Teeka just smiled when she looked at all of us back home together maybe for the last time. Momma Cye and Jaden cooked and we played cards drank wine and enjoyed each other's company. I always kept Marketta out of our family business so she didn't know about the fourth. I went back home that night and told her that I would be tied up for the holiday. She said it was fine because she promised her cousin she would come by. I spent all day Friday with Marketta and I talked to Terrance and Letha on the phone. I kissed Marketta, and kissed her stomach with my child in it. I held her tight before I left Saturday morning. She asked me.

"What's wrong RJ you act like you are not going to see us anymore."

"Nothing is wrong, I love you so much. I'm so happy you choose me to spend the rest of your life with. I guarantee to be their always for you and my child. I love you Marketta." She kissed me and left the softness of her lips on my mind as I drove away. When I reached the house I saw a white van in the drive way. I'd never saw the van before and I pulled out my gun and dialed Letha's cell. I didn't get an answer. My heart started beating fast and my adrenaline started flowing. I opened the door with my gun pointed in front of me. One guy had his back to me. The cold barrel on my gun touched his temple before I turned the corner to enter the room. The man froze and when I came in the room everybody watched my movement. Aunt Teeka smiled.

"RJ put the gun up. They are here to help us."

"Letha why you didn't answer your phone?" Letha looked on the table and found her phone. She told me she didn't know it was ringing. I put my gun up and I know I must have looked like a fool. But it showed I was always thinking about protecting my family. The guys that came in the truck brought us some uniforms made sure we had enough to fit then they left. I was confused. Aunt Teeka explained that the Gucci family has their meals catered. They loved barbeque ribs but don't know how to make them so they hire a company to cook for them and serve them. We were going to pose as the caterers to gain access inside the house. Momma Cye, Aunt Teeka, Terrance, Jada and I will pose as caterers and cooks. Aunt Teeka warned us not to eat any of the food. Jaden came downstairs and sat on Letha's lap. Letha smiled and nobody judged them. We were happy because they were happy. Jada hugged her sister for her strength she has and whispered in her ear.

"Today is the day we get even, so we can move on with our life's. I love you sis."

"I love you too, Jaden." All this was getting a little teary eyed for me. We weren't going to a funeral so I hoped. We spent the next few hours eating barbeque and slaw. We talked about names for our babies. I knew my son's name would be Reginald Johnson III, Terrance didn't really care. He just wanted his baby and Jada to be in good health. He kissed Jada and rubbed her belly. Momma Cye said it's time to get ready. I was more than ready. I wanted to end this phase of my life. I was ready to go away with Marketta and my child. I dreamed about living in a warm weather climate. Where it didn't snow and was warm year around. We all went to the cellar in the basement. Aunt Teeka made all of us wear bullet proof vest under our clothes. We all got two guns with silences on them. I got two guns and an extra one that I put on my ankle. Jaden was in amazement. She hadn't even been in this part of the house. She looked around smiled to herself then said.

"I missed all of this while I was I school?"

"Yes little sister you did. Thank God." I said and tighten the vest around her body. She picked up a gun and I asked her if she knew how to use it. She said she had lessons from her mother so I knew she knew how. Momma Cye had bought a black van and a black sedan. Jaden and Letha got in the sedan and the rest of us got in the van. We drove to Bloomfield in silence. Each person in deep thought. We pulled the van to the back of the house and started the grill up. Aunt Teeka warned us to play it by ear. When we see an opportunity we will move then. Terrance and I watched the meat and the back of the house. Momma Cye and Aunt Teeka were in the kitchen cooking the sides to the meal. Jaden and Letha waited down the street because it was too early for guest to arrive. After an hour Letha called me and said that Jaden saw Leon come in the house with his sister Dena and another gentleman. She couldn't see the other guys face. Letha said she was going to wait until more guests arrived. Inside Jada tried to stay clear of Dena and her brother. Her and Terrance took at walk in the large backyard that was by a lake. When more guests arrived Jaden and Dena came in. Dena saw her and rushed up and hugged her. Jaden introduced Letha to Dena. Letha had to fake a smile and be pleasant. Her brother was down in the basement with his guest. Dena took them around and introduced them to her family. Jaden didn't remember anybodies name other than they were Gucci's. Letha just nodded when introduced not wanting to touch anybodies hand. Momma Cye came in and served the guest making sure she gave eye contact to her daughter reassuring her that we were watching everything she did. The guest ate some hodurbs and Dena invited Letha and Jaden to go downstairs. Jada was on the other side of the room when she notice them go downstairs. She came outside and told Terrance and I told Aunt Teeka and Momma Cye.

"This is Leon my brother and this is Letha you know Jaden already, That's my cousin George." Letha tried to be cool and stay focus. She had to have Jaden back by any means necessary.

"Hi Jaden I been thinking about you."

"What have you been thinking about me?" Jaden tried not let her emotions show.

"Let me tell you." He pulled Jaden off to the side. Letha was watching with killer eyes. She wanted to pull her guns out and start blazing away. George tried to step to Letha and start a conversation. Letha listened to his weak rap but her eyes were on Jaden's every move. Dena was talking to the other guy downstairs. So it looked like we were coupled off. Letha saw Leon pull Jaden towards a room. If Jaden went in the room she would have to take the other three people out by herself. She reached for her gun as Leon reached the door knob. Someone came down the stairs.

"Jaden" someone yelled. Everybody turned to the staircase to see Jada standing their holding a tray of food. Leon looked at her then back at Jaden. Dena thought she was seeing things.

"Wait a minute who are you?" He asked Jada.

"I'm Jaden you don't remember me?" He looked at Jada then back at Jaden he couldn't tell.

"I would know my baby anywhere." Dena said looked at both girls then walked over to Jada and kissed her in the mouth. Jada wanted to kill her then but she let her kiss her for her sister's safety.

"This is my baby here I didn't know she had a twin." Leon looked at both of them. His imagination began to run on him as he pictured both girls in the bed naked while he fucked both.

"Which one of you two did I fuck?" He had plenty of balls. Jada started to blow his head off right then but her sister was too close. George had his hand on his gun it seemed to strange to be a coincident to him. The other guy didn't know what was going on. He just looked.

"I'm the one you raped." Jada said looking hard at Leon across the room. Leon hand a smirk on his face as he pictured having Jaden helpless while he violated her in every way imaginable sexually. He put his hand on his crouch proud of what he did to her. He looked at both girls trying to decide which one he would fuck first. Jaden eyed him.

"I am the one you raped and it wasn't good." She reached in her pocket with her right hand. In one swift motion she stuck the sharp ice pick through his hand the was on his crouch. The ice pick was ten inches long and it went through to penetrate his penis. Leon screamed in pain. Jaden turned to face him pulling her left hand up with a 9 millimeter pistol in it. She didn't hesitate to put the gun to his head and pull the trigger. In the few sections that it took Dena ran up the stairs. Jada had to cover her sister whose back was to George as he pulled out his gun. Jada fired from under the tray she was carrying and the bullets caught George off guard. Three red spots showed on his white shirt. His body fell over and hit the end table. The glass shattered making a lot of noise. The other guy stood looking until Letha put him down with two bullets to the head. Dena went upstairs screaming which caused Momma Cye and Aunt Teeka to come out shooting. The other family member ducked behind couches and returned fire. Terrance and I came around to the front door to make sure no one left. Shooting erupted in the vestibule when the girls came out the basement. Aunt Teeka was hit and went down. Letha screamed Mama then ran towards her mother and was hit twice. Her body spun around and she fell to the floor. Momma Cye ran over to Aunt Teeka firing at anything that moved. She continued shooting. Jaden ran over to Letha shooting all the way then she stopped. All of a sudden everybody stopped shooting. Someone was yelling and screaming. But the shooting stopped. Jaden hugged Letha as Terrance and I cautiously walked in the room with our guns up and ready to explode again.. The person screaming was Marketta. I was shocked and hurt. I saw blood on her body. I dropped my gun and walked over to her. Momma Cye held Aunt Teeka and cried. Jada went to her.

"Stop please stop this." I looked at Marketta shocked I didn't know what to do or think. "RJ this is my family. Please stop. I knew they were feuding with someone but not you. Please stop. Don't kill no more." She looked at the men behind the couches. "Uncle Leo please this is my baby's daddy. This is my family too. Please no more killing." She took a gun off the floor. "I will kill this seed in side of me that represents everyone in here." She said as tears ran down her face. She put the gun to her stomach. "If this doesn't stop"

"Wait Marketta you are my brother's child and I will not lose the only line of him I have left."

"Uncle Leo I love this man. We are going to make a life for ourselves and your nephew. Too many have died. I want my son to know both my families. I didn't meet most of my family because they are dead and for what? It's been twenty years since this started I won't put my son through another twenty years." Marketta put the gun to her stomach and pulled the trigger. I tried to catch her hand. Uncle Leo tackled her. All three of us fell to the ground. I pushed Uncle Leo off me to get to Marketta and my unborn son. I just knew they were dead. I grabbed her face. The gun somehow didn't go off. I helped Marketta off the floor and I noticed some water. She looked at me and smiled.

"My water broke. It's time to have your son." Tears of joy were in my eyes. I picked up the gun she had and threw it on the floor. I took the gun out my ankle holster and threw it on the floor. Jaden took Letha's gun and hers and threw them on the pile. One by one all the Gucci family members threw their guns on the pile on the floor. Terrance and Jada put their guns up. They still didn't trust the Gucci's. Momma Cye walked over to the pile with tears in her eyes. She looked at all the Gucci family members with tears running down her face. She threw her two guns on the floor and walked out the house. Marketta was having contractions. I picked her up and took her out to the car. Terrance picked up Aunt

Teeka and took her to the van. Jada and Jaden helped Letha to the car and we all rushed to the hospital. We knew that was this was the end. We would see the Gucci's again but next time on different terms. Life is funny I had a baby by the daughter of the guy that killed my mother. I'm part of the family that killed my uncle, cousin and grandparents. There were plenty of lives wasted on this feud. At least I know it won't follow any of the families to 'The Next Generation.'

The End

Other books by Mark Saint Cyr

Mama Raised A Killer

Mama Raised A Killer, The Revenge

Mama Raised A Killer, Finale

Mark Saint Cyr

Author Bio:

Mark Saint Cyr was born and raised in Detroit on the North end. He watched pimps, prostitutes, drug dealers and dope fiends infiltrate the community. He moved to New York as a teenager and lived in Harlem and the Bronx. Living in rough neighborhoods gave him firsthand knowledge of urban street life. He returned to Detroit with his artistic craft of writing. The street savvy and vivid reality he pens in his books "Mama Raised A Killer, Mama Raised a Killer, The Revenge and Mama Raised A Killer, The Finale" had readers waiting for more. He lived the street life and survived to write about it.

All Books available at:

Athtechpublishing.com

Amazon.com

Send reviews to mrkii@att.net

A Division of Atg Technologies & Filmworks, LLC